point

The Addams Family

A novelization by Elizabeth Faucher
from the screenplay
Written by Caroline Thompson & Larry Wilson
Based on the Characters created by Charles Addams

SCHOLASTIC INC.
New York Toronto London Auckland Sydney

PARAMOUNT PICTURES PRESENTS A SCOTT RUDIN PRODUCTION ANJELICA HUSTON RAUL JULIA CHRISTOPHER LLOYD THE ADDAMS FAMILY MUSIC BY MARC SHAIMAN DIRECTOR OF PHOTOGRAPHY OWEN ROIZMAN, A.S.C. PRODUCTION DESIGNED BY RICHARD MacDONALD EDITED BY DEDE ALLEN, A.C.E. COSTUME DESIGNER RUTH MYERS CO-PRODUCER JACK CUMMINS EXECUTIVE PRODUCER GRAHAM PLACE WRITTEN BY CAROLINE THOMPSON & LARRY WILSON BASED ON THE CHARACTERS CREATED BY CHARLES ADDAMS PRODUCED BY SCOTT RUDIN DIRECTED BY BARRY SONNENFELD

A PARAMOUNT COMMUNICATIONS COMPANY

These credits are tentative and subject to change.

ISBN 0-590-45541-9

12 11 10 9 8 7 6   2 3 4 5 6/9

Printed in the U.S.A.   01

First Scholastic printing, December 1991

Chapter 1

The house had no welcome mat. No brightly colored Christmas lights. No smiling family in the doorway, inviting everyone to come in, sit by the fire, and drink some nice, fresh eggnog.

The house *did* have a heavy iron gate, crooked front steps, more than a few gaping jagged holes where there should have been windows — and there was a big black wreath nailed up on the old wooden door.

It was the sort of house where devils would fear to tread.

But, the group of dauntless neighborhood carolers, more stubbornly cheerful than Girl Scouts on parade, lifted their voices in song, gathered in a tight semicircle of good fellowship. They sang — loudly, proudly — "The Little Drummer Boy," and when there was no response from the occupants of the dark house, they sang it again, heartier and happier than ever.

And again.

And *again*.

Up on the roof, the Addams family — Gomez, Morticia, Granny, Pugsley, Wednesday, and Lurch, their faithful butler, looked down at the beaming singers as they went into yet another deafening and enthusiastic verse of "The Little Drummer Boy." Slowly, they pushed their cauldron of bubbling, steaming pitch closer to the edge and then, with one gleeful push, tipped it over onto the carolers below.

It was the traditional Addams family holiday greeting.

The Addams family always liked to get up early. Start the day off *right*. Promptly at seven A.M., the cuckoo clock in the upstairs hallway, which was a perfect replica of the Addams family house, right down to the creaking shutters, chimed the hour.

In one window, a little mechanical Gomez moved a mechanical Morticia back until she was almost off her feet, and then bent to give her *one, two, three* mechanical kisses, counting down towards seven o'clock. In another window, a mechanical Pugsley hung a mechanical Wednesday from a noose on a gallows, up and down — *four, five* — while — *six* — little bursts of fog floated off the rooftop, where a tiny mechanical Granny was cranking her fog machine. The front door popped open — *seven* — and a little mechanical Lurch appeared to sweep the front steps.

After the seventh chime, Thing, the disembodied hand with the full-bodied personality, climbed over from the back of the clock, and leapt to the floor. He scampered down the hall, moving so fast that he went right past a pair of legs in pajamas, the feet of which were clad in bedroom slippers. Thing skidded to an instant halt and scampered back to the legs, pulling on the left cuff of the pajama bottoms.

The legs, of course, belonged to Gomez, who was standing in the hallway, staring mournfully into his long-lost brother Fester's bedroom. He was wearing a fez and a smoking jacket over his pajamas and, despite the fact that it was only seven in the morning, puffing away on one of his beloved cigars.

"Think of it, Thing," he said, with a sigh that radiated unfathomable woe. "He's been gone for twenty-five years. For twenty-five *years*, we've attempted to contact Fester in the great beyond, and for twenty-five years, *nothing*."

The room was a dusty, cobweb-filled shrine to Fester, untouched since his disappearance as a teenager. Nothing had ever been moved, or cleaned — from the Alcatraz football pennant, to the headless sports trophies, to the high school class picture in which all the other students kept as much distance from Fester as possible.

"Twenty-five years," Gomez said sadly, "and not a whisper. Not a clue. I'm beginning to think my brother truly is lost." He sighed again and took a mournful puff on his cigar.

Thing tugged at Gomez' cuff, pulling him down the hallway. Then, the little hand scampered ahead and flung himself up onto an old-fashioned door latch and opened the door into Gomez and Morticia's bedroom.

Morticia lay asleep on the bed, on black satin sheets. Quiet and incisive, she was rarely one to smile, and her skin looked even more ghostly white than usual, framed by the black of the pillowcase and her black hair, which was spread out around her face like a diabolic halo.

"Look at her," Gomez said, barely breathing. "I would die for her. I would *kill* for her. Either way — what bliss."

Morticia, ever sultry and remote, opened her eyes.

"Unhappy, darling?" Gomez asked adoringly.

"Oh, yes, *yes*," Morticia said, with great passion. "*Completely*."

Which was their favorite way to say good morning.

Down the hall, Pugsley was crouched on the floor in his room, playing with his chemistry set. His bedroom walls were covered with road signs he had collected — BRIDGE OUT, DETOUR: EXCAVATION AHEAD, DANGEROUS UNDERTOW, KEEP CLEAR, and HIGH VOLTAGE. Sawed-off Stop signs, still on their poles, were stacked up in the far corner.

On the other side of the room, there was a floor-to-ceiling fish tank, filled with ravenous man-eating fish, snapping at each other and at the glass encasing them.

In thought, word, and deed, it was clear that

Pugsley, a tubby, energetic nine year old, had every chance of growing up to be the public monster his parents would be proud of.

He mixed chemicals in a glass beaker, and then, when the brew began to steam, he grinned wickedly and gulped it down. Almost instantly, his body began to contort, undergoing the beginnings of a transformation, and then, he shrank to the size of a mouse.

Laughing, he climbed out of his human-sized pajamas. He wanted to be able to cause as much damage and fright as possible before the spell wore off.

Up in the attic, Wednesday sat solemnly on a small wooden stool, perched among the stored family objects. She was ten years old, with her mother's jet-black hair and pale white skin. She sat very still, one end of a string tied to her tooth, the other tied to a trapdoor.

The trapdoor suddenly slammed open, and Granny — a truly frightful and giggly old hag — poked her head up to see Wednesday's pulled tooth swinging at the end of the string.

"Thank you, Grandmama," Wednesday said gravely.

Granny grumbled something unintelligible and stomped up into the attic, her hair so frizzy that it looked as if she had been in a bathtub when the hair dryer fell in.

"You kids are going to have to kill your own breakfast this morning," she said grumpily.

Wednesday nodded and opened the small cigar

box on her lap. Inside, she had various human and animal teeth, fangs and dentures, along with a collection of glass eyes.

This new, still bloody, tooth would be a lovely addition to her collection.

So far, every member of the Addams family was having an absolutely perfect morning.

Chapter 2

Still up in their bedroom, Gomez took Morticia into his arms. As she languidly draped herself across his chest, she was caught in a sudden shaft of sunlight. She squinted, and cringed away from it, and the huge, carnivorous orchid on the bedside table next to her wilted.

"Gomez," she said, her voice faint. "The sun. *Il me perce comme un poignard.*"

"Tish," Gomez said, wildly excited, "that's French!"

"*Oui,*" Morticia said, and shrugged nonchalantly.

"*Cara mia!*" He kissed his way up her neck and then, bursting with enthusiasm and a sense of purpose, jumped up from the bed, drawing his bedside saber from its sheath and brandished it at the offending sunbeam. "*En garde, Monsieur soleil!*" he shouted, and thrust and parried with the sword, pantomiming a duel with the shaft of light.

"Gomez?" Morticia asked, her hand trailing weakly off the side of the bed.

He kept slashing away with his sword. "*Querida?*" he asked.

"Last night, you were . . . unhinged," she said, examining the blood-red of her nail polish. "You were like some desperate, howling demon. You frightened me." She paused, then managed a wan smile. "Do it *again*."

He cast away his sword and returned to her at once.

Up on the roof, Granny gave her fog machine a vicious kick.

"Lousy bucket of bolts!" she said.

The fog machine, clanky and cumbersome, was malfunctioning, struggling to churn out its patches of thick fog, and she kicked it again, even harder.

At his bedroom window, Gomez stuck his head out while, behind him, Morticia sat at her dressing table, brushing her hair with a silver filigree brush.

"Granny," he called up to the roof, quite disturbed. "Where's your fog?"

The only answer he got was the fog machine hurtling downwards, which missed decapitating him by mere millimeters. The machine smashed through the porch roof and crashed to the ground.

Gomez looked at the mess of machinery, then shrugged, and closed the window.

Lurch, the gigantic family butler, was standing just inside the front door, holding two brown paper lunch bags in his enormous hands for the children to take to school. The bags' contents squirmed and wriggled, eager to escape.

Wednesday, on her way out, reached up to take her bag. "Thank you, Lurch," she said.

Pugsley — back to his normal pudgy size — took his bag, opening it to peer inside. Lurch growled at him, and Pugsley quickly closed the bag and followed his sister outside.

Lurch didn't like it when the Addams children were late to school. He didn't like it at all.

Upstairs, Gomez now stood on the balcony outside his bedroom practicing his golf swing. He hit ball after ball, with Thing serving as his golf tee. Morticia sat behind them, watching, and sipping her morning cup of tea.

One of the golf balls flew, with incredible speed, through the window of the Addams family's only neighbor, the grouchy old Judge Womack. Judge Womack lived in the beautifully tended, elegant house up on the hill overlooking the Addamses' mansion. As the ball crashed through his kitchen window, Judge Womack looked up from his breakfast just in time to see the ball land in his cornflakes and shatter the bowl, covering him with splattered milk.

Furious, Judge Womack ran over to the broken window, shaking his fist in frustration.

"Addams!" he shouted.

From the balcony, it looked to Gomez and Morticia as though the Judge were waving at them — so they waved back.

"Sorry about the window, Judge!" Gomez yelled over. "Keep the ball! I have a whole bucketful." He held up his bucket as evidence of this, then tossed his golf club to Thing, who deposited it in Gomez' golf bag.

Out in front of the house, the school bus was just pulling away.

"The little ones, off to school," Morticia said fondly. "Bless them."

Gomez nodded. "They grow up so fast, don't they?"

"*Too* fast," Morticia said, and they both smiled with pride as the school bus strained to chug down the road, tires smoking. Pugsley hung onto the rear bumper, grinning fiendishly and dragging his heels.

Morticia and Gomez had a very pleasant morning in the conservatory. Morticia, wearing her nicest gardening gloves and humming a little, tended to her roses, methodically cutting off each and every blossom with a pair of shiny shears.

Gomez sat at a small table, out of the sunshine, playing chess with Thing. He made a bold move, then looked over at his wife.

"It's a milestone, Tish," he said. "This very evening — our twenty-fifth séance. All these years, gnawed by guilt, undone by woe, burning with uncertainty . . ."

"Oh, Gomez." Morticia snipped off another flower, leaving a long ugly stalk on the bush. "Don't torture yourself. That's *my* job."

The thought of that made Gomez smile. Widely.

"Imagine, darling," Morticia said, snipping away, "if Fester did come back. Half alive, barely human, a rotting shell — "

Since that was his very fondest wish, Gomez sighed. "Don't tease," he said. Because the thought of Fester's return was too wonderful to contemplate.

It would be a dream come true.

Chapter 3

Just outside the Addamses' property, Tully Alford, the family attorney, and his wife, Margaret, approached "Gate," a wrought iron monstrosity that always opened of its own accord.

Or not.

Tully, who had once been handsome and was now puffy and middle-aged, stopped in front of Gate, looking up at the house without enthusiasm.

"Well, come *on*," Margaret said, moving ahead of him. A high-strung and superficial woman, she spent almost all of her waking hours being disappointed in, and by, her husband.

As Tully followed her through Gate, Gate slammed unexpectedly, clipping him and catching the end of his coat. Yanked to an immediate halt, Tully tried to pull his coat free, fighting with Gate.

"Let go!" Tully said, tugging as hard as he could. "Gimme that! *Stop* it!" He kept pulling without success. "I'm warning you, Gate! It's *not* a good day!"

Inside the conservatory, Gomez moved a chess piece and then, as Thing gestured dramatically towards the window, he and Morticia both looked out. As they did, Thing quickly moved *two* chess pieces, cheating.

"Look, darling," Morticia said. "Tully is here."

Gomez laughed, watching the struggle in the yard. "Ha! That Tully," he said, and shook his head.

Morticia nodded, also bemused. "Romping with Gate again."

Gomez returned his attention to the chess board and made a move. "Check," he said.

Thing made his own move, and then gestured in triumph, while Gomez frowned.

"Checkmate," Morticia said, very impressed. "Good for you, Thing."

Gomez just frowned, and set the pieces up to play again. For some reason, whenever they played chess, Thing *always* won.

Outside, halfway up the front walk, Margaret stopped impatiently.

"Tully!" she said, and stamped her foot. "Can't you keep up?"

Tully ripped his coat, attempting to get it away from Gate. "I'm *trying*," he said.

Margaret put her hands on her hips, very displeased. "These are your *last* paying clients, may I remind you!"

"If it gives you pleasure," Tully said, and ripped his coat completely, finally getting away.

"Yes, well, *something* has to," Margaret said. She looked down at her rather unfashionable outfit. "Like a decent coat, say. Something dressy, for evening. Ask — for a loan. *Beg*."

Tully shook his head. "No loans! I'm not a bum!" Then he nodded, cutting his wife off before she could respond. "Don't say it. I'll get the money," he promised. "I have a plan."

Margaret put her hand to her forehead. "This is all so humiliating," she said. "Why did I marry you?"

Tully shrugged. "Because I said yes."

Margaret ignored that and marched on towards the front door, neatly skirting the fog machine as if it had every reason in the world to be there.

The machine hissed at Tully as he passed it, spurting fog all over his trousers. Tully jumped away from it and hurried up the porch steps.

They were met in the front entryway by an unsmiling Lurch. Tully handed him his hat and what was left of his coat and headed for Gomez' study. Finding herself alone with the giant butler, Margaret was more nervous and intimidated than she would ever admit.

"I-I'm here to see Mrs. Addams," she said, with false confidence. "About the charity auction."

With a low grunt, Lurch headed for the stairs. Screwing up her courage, Margaret followed him.

As Tully walked glumly down the hall to the study, he passed the Addams family portraits — generations of Addams grotesques, in elaborate gilt frames. Staring at the horrible pictures, Tully didn't notice the bear rug on the floor and stepped right on it.

The bear rug growled a ferocious growl, clamping its jaws onto his trouser leg. Tully shouted in pain, dancing around, and finally managed to shake off the rug. Once he was sure he was safe, he looked up, only to find himself face-to-face with a portrait of the teenage Fester Addams. The painting was draped in black crepe and holding a lit candle.

Exactly *how* it was holding the lit candle was a complete mystery.

The portrait was Fester, at fifteen, completely hairless, with a dead white complexion and eyes rimmed in black like a raccoon's. The identifying plaque below read: "Fester Addams, 1947–?"

Tully studied the picture intently, almost as if he were having a premonition. But then, the intricately carved doors leading to Gomez' study creaked open. Tully took a deep breath and went inside.

As he stepped into the room, a sword sliced through the air, its blade glinting in the light from the chandelier. Tully grabbed for the hilt, and missed. The blade embedded itself in the wall next to him with a shuddering *thunk*.

Gomez, who was standing by the mantlepiece, laughed. "Missed," he said. Then, he leapt across the room, brandishing his own saber.

Tully backpedaled and, as he pulled the sword from the wall, he pointed at something behind Gomez. "What's that?!"

Gomez turned to see, and Tully charged, wielding the sword, swinging for Gomez' throat.

Gomez parried the blow easily. "Dirty pool, old man," he said. "I *like* it!" He drove Tully back, with swift slashes, shredding his jacket to pieces.

"Had enough?" Tully asked, out of breath.

Gomez just laughed and they continued to fence.

15

Gomez flipped open Tully's briefcase with his sword, and a sheaf of legal papers spilled out.

"Where's my pen?" Gomez asked. "Never mind — I'll use yours." His blade found the pen in Tully's inside jacket pocket, flipped it out, and up into the air. He caught the pen, then did hand-springs back to his desk, landing gracefully in his chair. "*First*, the old business!" he said, swiveled in his chair to ward off another blow, then cavalierly continued the duel as he signed the legal documents scattered on the desk before him.

There was no reason that business and pleasure couldn't be *combined*.

Once they heard about the charity auction, Morticia and Granny took Margaret upstairs to look for just the right donation. They sorted through various Addams family possessions packed in trunks, stacked in boxes, and covered with ominous shrouds.

"Perhaps it's in here," Morticia said, and opened a large, elaborately carved armoire.

Granny giggled. "I don't think so . . ."

In the front of the armoire, there was an over-stuffed garment bag labeled "Uncle Niknak's Winter Clothes."

"Uncle Niknak's winter wardrobe," Morticia said, full of happy memories the second she saw it. She carefully passed the bag to Granny, who chucked it aside.

The next garment bag was marked "Uncle Niknak's Summer Clothes."

"Uncle Niknak's *summer* wardrobe," Morticia said, happily. She very gently passed the bag to Granny, who threw it on the floor.

Next in the armoire, there was a body bag.

"*Ahhh*," Morticia said, and beamed. "Uncle Niknak." She carefully lifted the bag and handed it to Granny, who handed it to Margaret — who fought off a scream.

Visiting the Addams family was always an adventure.

Chapter 4

Down in the study, the duel continued. Gomez, who hadn't even broken a sweat, fought away, still signing papers.

"I wish you'd drop by more often," he said.

Tully doggedly fought on, his jacket almost completely shredded now. "I'd like to," he said "but — "

"But what, old sport?" Gomez asked.

"Oh," Tully made himself keep swinging, "you know . . ."

"You know *what*?" Gomez asked.

Tully sighed. "I'm a bleeder."

Gomez laughed, then stopped dead, staring at one of the documents. Deftly, he disarmed Tully, sending his saber flying up into the air.

"What's this?" he asked. "A new proposal? 'The Fester Addams Offshore Retirement Fund'?" He frowned. "What would they do?"

"What *wouldn't* they do," Tully said, straightening his tie, and the shreds of his jacket. "It's a very worthy cause and a great addition to the Fester Addams funds."

"Fester — all tribute to thee," Gomez said rhapsodically. Then, he looked over. "Some called him inhumanly evil."

"No!" Tully protested.

"Only our parents," Gomez assured him. "I called him — brother."

"And his memory must live on, forever," Tully said quickly. "Through money. We'll deposit the funds under my name, for tax purposes."

"Really?" Gomez thought about that, then nodded. "It's inspired!"

"He would have wanted it that way," Tully said, pressing his advantage. "Beloved Fester."

"Indeed!" Gomez said, and tossed his sword back to Tully so that they could resume the duel. "For Fester!"

"For Fester!" Tully said. "A brother!"

"*My* brother!" Gomez said.

"One of a kind!" Tully proclaimed.

Gomez nodded. "The doctors all said!"

"Kind to animals!" Tully thrust. Parried. "So good with children!"

"They never proved anything," Gomez said quickly.

Tully swung his head, and missed. "One million dollars," he said. "The perfect amount."

Gomez nodded. "It's brilliant!"

"It's *untraceable*," Tully said.

Gomez paused for a second, lowering his sword. "But, Tully, it's not old business. It's going to have to wait. You know the rules better than that."

"What?" Tully was taken aback, his sword hand dropping to his side. "But this is different! It's in my name. Make an exception!"

Gomez shook his head. "Old business is old business, and new business is new business, and *this* . . ." he held up the proposal " . . . is *new* business, and we don't discuss new business until . . ." He stopped, rifling through a desk calendar with one finger, flipping endless pages. "Next quarter."

Tully paled. "*Next* quarter?!" he said, and charged with his sword like an enraged bull.

Gomez did a kung fu back flip out of his chair, and just missed being run through by Tully's saber. The saber skewered the overstuffed chair and, carried by the momentum of the charge, Tully somersaulted over the desk, collided with the chair, and landed on the floor with a heavy thud.

"Fine lunge," Gomez said, "but your riposte — a bit rusty." He carelessly flung away his sword, and Thing, perched up on a decorative samurai helmet, plucked the sword from the air and resheathed it. "Make yourself comfortable, old man," Gomez said to Tully, after nodding his thanks to Thing. "I'll get the money for the monthly expenses."

Tully, lying on the floor in a panting ruined heap, didn't answer.

Gomez picked up Tully's briefcase and made a brisk exit, closing the office doors behind him.

Tully crawled over to the doors, sliding them open a crack so he could spy on Gomez. He peeked into the den, watching as Gomez reached for a book (the title was *Greed*), pulling it partway from the shelf. The entire shelf — a secret panel — revolved and deposited Gomez on the other side of the wall before returning to its original position.

Intrigued, Tully got to his feet, went through the doors, and staggered over to the bookcase. Behind it, he could hear Gomez making his descent down into the vault, with the sounds of chains and pulleys, creaking and groaning, and vague animal howls.

He *wanted* to get in there — but, then again, maybe he didn't.

. Morticia emptied the entire armoire without finding what she wanted, so she checked a nearby shelf. Thing, upstairs now, offered her a bejeweled treasure.

"There it is," she said. "Just what we've been searching for." She took the treasure. "Thank you, Thing." She passed Margaret the jewel-encrusted cylinder of webbed gold dragon's heads with gaping jaws at either end.

At first, Margaret was afraid to touch it, but her innate greed helped her to get over this.

"What is it?" she asked, in awe.

Morticia looked at it proudly. "A family heirloom. A finger trap from the court of Emperor Wu."

"It must be worth a *fortune*," Margaret breathed. "Look at those emeralds. Oh, Morticia, this is just *too* extravagant," she said, without much conviction. "Even for the auction."

Granny nodded, in complete agreement. "Let's keep it."

"Hush," Morticia said. "It's for charity. Widows and orphans. We need *more* of them! Margaret?"

Enchanted by the object, Margaret wasn't listening. She inserted her fingers in the trap . . . and got stuck. "Mmmm?" she said, struggling to get free.

"The séance, tonight," Morticia said. "Won't you come? It's Gomez. I'm terribly worried. He won't eat, he can't sleep, he's been coughing up blood . . ."

Margaret stared at her in horror. "He coughs up *blood*?"

"Well . . . not like he used to . . ." Morticia said sadly.

Tully stood in front of the bookcase in the den, reaching for a book, from approximately the same place where Gomez had unlocked the secret panel. But — nothing happened.

Frowning, Tully looked at the title — *Gone With the Wind* — and then opened the cover. A hurricane blast of wind gusted from the open book, blowing Tully's hair straight up, and rippling his facial muscles. He managed to close the book and, heart pounding, returned it to the shelf.

Lurch had been watching him from the hall, where he was dusting, and Tully grinned sheepishly at him.

Lurch was not amused.

A few minutes later, Gomez came back up to the study, setting Tully's briefcase, now full of greenish-gold doubloons, on his desk. Carefully, he counted them, wearing an accountant's eyeshade, and weighing each handful of coins on an old-fashioned measuring scale before returning them to the case.

"There," he said, finally. "The monthly expenses."

Tully snapped the briefcase shut and hoisted it from Gomez' desk. It was dead weight in his hand — the usual monthly ordeal for him.

"I, uh, I don't suppose you have any paper money in the vault," he said, trying to be polite. "Gomez, it's time. For the new fund. A *checkbook*."

Gomez shook his head. "Never! The banks — I don't trust them." He lowered his voice. "Strange people, Tully. Not like you and me. Or — Fester. Oh!" He straightened up. "The séance! I need you here. For him."

"Séance?" Tully said doubtfully, lugging the briefcase towards the door.

Gomez nodded. "Eight o'clock. Sharp. And, by the way . . ."

Tully turned back, and Gomez flipped an extra doubloon across the room, right into Tully's vest pocket.

"I broke another of Judge Womack's windows this morning," Gomez said.

Tully nodded, sighed his biggest sigh, and headed for the door.

Judge Womack was, as always, going to be just *thrilled* to see him.

Chapter 5

Judge Womack was *so* thrilled to see Tully that he wouldn't even let him into the house. So, Tully stayed out on the front steps, fishing inside his vest pocket for the doubloon.

"Still working for Addams?" Judge Womack asked grumpily, then frowned at Margaret, who was standing on the front lawn. "Mother warned you, Margaret. I can still hear her voice, clear as a bell. She'd always say, day in, and day out, 'Marry Tully Alford — ' "

" 'And you'll hear Satan laugh,' " Tully finished, and tossed him the coin. "Here's your doubloon."

"I'm stuck!" Margaret said, still struggling with the finger trap.

Judge Womack gave Tully a dirty look, apparently suspecting that he had put the trap on her. "You *lowlife*," he said, then examined the jeweled treasure more closely. "Oh, my. Are those emeralds?"

Margaret nodded, and the Judge was quick to

come down the steps and help her. To admire, and covet, the emeralds.

After leaving the Judge's house, Tully went back to his law office, lugging his impossibly heavy briefcase. His offices had once been quite fancy, but now the leather on the chairs was starting to crack, and a repainting was long overdue.

He stopped in the front alcove, looking around for his secretary. "Miss Bradbury?" He looked around some more. "Miss Bradbury!"

"She's at lunch, Mr. Alford," a voice said from his office.

Since there wasn't supposed to be anyone in there, Tully frowned, stepping cautiously inside.

There, sitting in the client's chair in front of his desk, was Abigail Craven, an arrogant old woman in her sixties. Her steely will and conniving manipulativeness were barely veiled by a very thin layer of polish and good manners.

Tully forced a smile, setting down his briefcase.

"Mrs. Craven, I was about to call you," he said.

Abigail just sniffed. "I'm certain you were," she said, then gestured to her right. "You haven't met my son, Gordon, have you, Mr. Alford?"

Tully turned, ready with a pleasant smile, but when he caught sight of Gordon his face fell. Gordon, a fleshy and round man in his forties, was impeccably, if eccentrically, dressed. His dark hair was plastered to his head with pomade, and with his barrel chest and kamikaze demeanor, he was a threatening sight, indeed.

"Is this the one, Mother?" Gordon asked. "The deadbeat you mentioned?"

Before Tully could react, Gordon had him by the throat, hanging him upside down from the wall like an oil painting.

"Wait a minute, hold on!" Tully said, choking. "You have to listen to me!"

"We do, Mr. Alford?" Abigail smiled meanly. "And why is that?"

"Please," Tully said, gasping. "Just hear me out . . ."

Gordon looked over at his mother and shrugged. "Mother . . . your call."

Abigail smiled at him. "Gordon and I enjoy a very . . . special relationship," she said to Tully. "I'm *wild* about him."

"She's a pip," Gordon said, nodding cheerfully.

"Refreshing, no?" Abigail said, then looked at Tully's strained, panicked face. "Down, Gordon."

Gordon looked very disappointed. "*Mother . . .*"

"Gordon," his mother said sharply.

"Gordon!" Tully said, his voice coming out in a croak.

Gordon sighed, then let go, dropping Tully on his head. Whimpering, Tully crawled towards his desk.

"And how is your wife, Mr. Alford?" Abigail asked, her hands neatly folded in her lap. "I've heard so much about her. Still charming? Still . . . *spending*?"

"I don't have the money to repay you," Tully said, weakly. "I've tried everything."

"Yes, well, we've lent you a considerable sum," Abigail said, brushing a tiny piece of lint from her sleeve. "Many thousands of dollars. Payment due. Now."

Tully nodded. "Soon, I promise."

Abigail studied him, then shook her head with mock sadness. "Oh, Gordon, I *want* to believe him."

"So do I," Gordon said, and showed Tully his teeth.

"He's so terribly trusting," Abigail said to Tully.

"She's a *saint*," Gordon said to Tully.

Tully just nodded uneasily, looking from one to the other.

Abigail smiled again at her son. "Silly boy. Make me proud."

Gordon grabbed Tully and swept him up onto his desk. As he did, Tully's briefcase popped open, and the doubloons spilled out. Seeing the gold, Abigail and Gordon exchanged a malicious smile.

"He lied to us, Mother," Gordon said.

"No!" Tully said, close to hysteria. "It's not what you think! Those are doubloons! For the Addams account!"

Abigail put a thoughtful finger to her forehead. "Addams?"

"There's more," Tully said desperately. "There's a fortune, but no one can get to it! Don't you think I've tried?"

"Have you?" Abigail asked. "Have you tried hard enough?" She turned to her son. "Ask him, sweetheart."

Gordon took a menacing step forward.

"No!" Tully lifted his arms to try and protect himself. "Sweetheart! *Don't* ask!"

Gordon's face hovered just inches from his own. The glare from the light bulb hanging overhead whited out his hair, making him look bald as a cue ball. Making him look just like — Tully stared at him, in disbelief.

Gordon was the spitting image of the long-lost Fester.

Chapter 6

It was dark, and Morticia stood at the open window in the den, watching a terrible thunderstorm. Lightning flashed, thunder roared, rain swirled around — and she was enjoying every second.

Gomez stood behind her, his arms around her waist. "Hailstones," he said dreamily.

"And lightning," Morticia said.

Gomez nodded. "It's a miserable night."

"I know, darling. Beautiful séance weather." Morticia leaned out the window. "Children, come on inside now! We're starting!" Then she laughed. "And put down that antenna!"

Just as she said that there was another crackling flash of lightning. . . .

Across town, Gordon and Abigail were in a run-down highway-style motel room with stained plastic curtains and a splotchy oil painting. Gordon was sitting on the bed, facing a cracked mirror. Abigail stood to one side, consulting a picture of Fester that Tully had lent them, looking from it to the mirror.

"It's uncanny," she said. "My little boy, and this *hideous* creature."

"Mother," Gordon protested, his feelings hurt.

"Uh, handsome creation," Abigail said, and smiled at him. "Think of it, my angel. No more grubby storefront scams. No more loansharking to scum like Tully Alford. All that delicious money — I can *feel* it, right in my fingertips."

"So can I," Gordon said, his hands opening and closing automatically.

Abigail put down the ugly picture, repressing a shudder. "Now, it's only one week, and out. You locate the vault, and then we're gone — *poof*! Before they notice what's missing."

"And Alford?" Gordon asked.

Abigail sighed. "We need him — for now. And later, we'll be miles away, and" — she grinned — "*he'll* take the rap."

Gordon grinned, too.

There was no way that the plan could fail.

When Tully and Margaret arrived at the Addamses' mansion for the séance, Lurch took their wet overcoats. Margaret was *still* stuck in the finger trap, so she had been unable to change her clothes — or do much of *anything*.

"What a miserable evening," she said grimly.

"Just don't add to it," Tully said.

Wednesday came out to escort them to the den.

"Big night for you guys!" Tully said heartily. "Hey, small fry?" He reached out to pat her head, but she moved out of the way.

"Hello, dear," Margaret said, with a tight smile pasted on her face, and then held up her trapped hands. "Could you?"

Wednesday deftly released her fingers from the trap — to Margaret's amazement.

"Thank you,"she said, and tried to straighten her disheveled clothes. "Call me a cab, Tully!"

Tully shook his head. "Get it yourself."

"Fine." Margaret held out her now-free hand impatiently. "Give me the car keys."

"Give it a *rest*," Tully said.

Morticia appeared in the doorway, looking ravishing and pale in black. "Welcome, honored guests."

Lurch presented a tray of vile-looking canapés.

"Entrails?" Morticia said, motioning to the tray.

Tully and Margaret shook their heads. Firmly.

Once pleasantries had been exchanged, the family, and the Alfords, sat down at a round table, a crystal ball in the center. Lurch was at the organ in the corner of the room, playing mood music — dramatic, crashing chords.

"Let us gather," Morticia said, "in this house of yearning, on this day of heartsick loss, at this table of woe." She looked around the table. "Is everyone comfortable?"

Everyone but the Alfords.

Morticia picked up a tarnished gold statuette.

"Sing, O spirits!" she chanted. "Harken, all souls! Every year on this date, we offer a clarion call to Fester Addams."

Wednesday kicked Pugsley under the table. "*Stop* it!"

"Pugsley . . ." Gomez scolded him.

Pugsley, who had a meat cleaver aimed at his sister, reluctantly handed it to Gomez, who smiled.

"*Kids*," he said to Tully, and set the cleaver aside.

Morticia raised the statuette high above her head. "From generation, to generation, our beacon to the beyond." Then, she passed the statuette to Wednesday. "Do you accept the glorious burden?"

Wednesday nodded, taking the statuette. "May it weigh me down, through all my melancholy years."

"All close eyes, and join hands," Morticia said.

Which they all did, Granny taking a very squeamish Margaret's hand.

"Ow!" Granny said. "*What* a *grip*!" She pulled away, leaving her "hand" behind, her sleeve suddenly empty. "My hand! She's got my hand!"

Left holding Thing, Margaret shrieked.

Granny and Pugsley both laughed appreciatively as Margaret tried to shake Thing off.

"Excuse me," Margaret said, starting to get up, her face ashen. "I — "

Tully pulled her back into her seat. "Sit down, pumpkin. Join the fun."

"Mama, you should know better," Morticia said, with great affection. "Thing — you're a handful."

Thing let go of Margaret's hand, and ran out.

Still chuckling, Granny took hold of Margaret's now-rigid hand with her real hand.

With a last look around the table to ensure that everyone had settled down, Morticia resumed the séance.

"Wednesday," she said, with a nod.

"Let us ransom you from the power of the grave," Wednesday said, reciting the incantation perfectly. "Tonight, O Death, let us be your plague."

Now, Morticia looked at Granny. "Mama?"

"I feel that he's near," Granny said. "Fester Addams, gather your strength and knock three times."

Incredibly, there was the heavy hollow sound of three knocks on the front door, reverberating through the house.

Granny's eyes popped open. "Did you hear *that*?!"

"Ask again, Mama," Morticia said. "Quickly."

Lurch played an inspiring, loud chord on the organ.

"By all means!" Tully said, knowing who it was out there, and barely able to contain his smug enthusiasm.

"Ask! Ask!" Gomez said urgently.

"Fester Addams — I demand that you knock again!" Granny said.

There were three hard knocks on the front door, Lurch hitting a crescendo on the organ in response.

Jubilant, Gomez sprang to his feet.

"He's here!" he said. "He's at the door!"

With the family right behind him, Gomez ran to the front door, eagerly pulling it open.

There, on the front steps, stood . . . *Fester*.

It was a miracle!

Chapter 7

Gordon did look convincing. Abigail had completely shaved his head, and his clothing and pallor were pure Fester. The exact resemblance was shocking.

He and Gomez stared at each other. Fester's eyes had a hard I-*dare*-you-to-question-me look in them. The two men just stared, neither one speaking.

"Could it be?" Morticia asked.

Granny moved closer to squint up at this sudden apparition. "Is that him?"

"Is it possible?" Tully asked, innocently.

"Good heavens," Margaret said, unable to take her eyes off the ugly sight.

Morticia looked at Gomez for confirmation. After all, twenty-five years was a long time. But, Gomez and Fester continued their face-off.

Finally, Gomez broke the stalemate. "Fester!" he said, throwing open his arms.

"Gomez!" Fester said, throwing open his arms a beat later.

Gomez smothered him in an embrace, which Fester endured.

Now, Abigail, who had been behind her transformed son, stepped forward. She had changed into a plain, dowdy suit, and her hair was in braided coils.

"Gut evenink," she said, in an assumed accent. "I am Dr. Pinder-Schloss."

Introductions were swiftly exchanged, and Morticia led everyone to the drawing room for snacks, and catching-up.

Fester stood by the tall, baronial fireplace, where an enormous fire was burning. Steam rose off his wet greatcoat, enveloping him. He was immobile, his black-ringed eyes ferretlike, and calculating.

Next to him, Pugsley examined the exotic labels on the steamer trunk Lurch had carried in for him.

"How did zis happen?" Abigail asked, seizing center stage. "How did it come to be? Ze story — it is most amazink, and also beautiful."

The Addams family sat down, eager to hear the tale.

"He vas found in Miami, tangled in ze tuna net!" Abigail explained. "It vas just last month, during ze Hurricane Helga. Ze sky, it vas black like pitch. Ze vaves, zey vere valls of doom." She paused. "Can you imagine?"

From the smiles on everyone's faces, it was obvious that they could, and *did*, imagine the charming scene.

"Zen," Abigail went on, "zey drag him from ze ocean, from ze very jaws of oblivion. I'm telling you! Zere are tests, so many tests, and a complete psychological profile. At long last, ze Florida Department of ze Fish unt ze Game, zey say, low and beholdt, my oh my, go tell it on ze mountaintop — he is . . . your bruzzer! Boom!"

Everyone jumped, then laughed delightedly, smiling over at the silent, steaming Fester.

"Zey gif him to me," Abigail said, "at Human Services, and I am bringink him, after all zese years, after who knows *vat* heartache, after ze naked and ze dead, I am bringink him *home to you!*"

Margaret shook her head, unconvinced. "That's preposterous," she said.

"Margaret . . ." Tully muttered, jabbing her in the ribs so she would be quiet.

"But, don't you think that's absurd?" Margaret asked.

"Honey . . ." Tully said, quietly.

"Isn't it the most *ridiculous* thing you've ever heard?" Margaret asked.

Tully gritted his teeth. "Blossom, *dear* . . ."

"It certainly is," Gomez said, and gave Fester a companionable slap.

Fester, who hated being touched, flinched away.

"And now, you're back," Gomez said, smiling.

Tully nodded. "Back to share your joys, back to share your sorrows, back to share — well, hey — everything!"

"I just don't know," Margaret said doubtfully.

Tully handed her the finger trap to distract her. "Darling, how does this work again?"

Margaret looked at him with disgust. "An *infant* would understand," she said — and demonstrated, promptly getting stuck again.

Morticia stretched out on the couch with languid joy. "Fester Addams, home at long last."

"Well, at least . . . for a week," Fester said.

Morticia stopped reclining. "Only a week?"

"Don't be ridiculous!" Gomez said. "You're home!"

Fester shook his head. "Sorry, but I have to get back. I've got a lot of things cooking in the, uh, Bermuda Triangle."

"Oh, Gomez," Morticia said, aglow with romance. "The Bermuda Triangle!"

"Devil's Island," Gomez said fondly.

"The Black Hole of Calcutta," Morticia said, her gaze and voice both wistful.

"Someday, dear," Gomez promised. "A second honeymoon."

At the steamer trunk, Pugsley was disintergrating the lock with a beakerful of acid and an eyedropper.

Morticia turned to Abigail. "Dr. Pinder-Schloss, will you be staying, too?"

"No, no," Abigail said. "I really must be goink. But, I vill be back, you can bet. To be checkink on Fester's adjustment."

The acid had eaten away the lock on Fester's trunk, and Pugsley opened the lid, reaching inside with one arm and fishing among the contents. There was a loud snap, and he grinned, pulling out his hand — which was crushed in a rusty bear trap.

"*Cool*," he said, admiring the destruction.

Wednesday stood alone, in the corner of the room, in her usual mournful fashion. She was instinctively suspicious of this new Fester.

"Nobody gets out of the Bermuda Triangle," she said. "Not even for a vacation. *Everyone* knows that."

Abigail looked at her pityingly. "Oh, my little vun," she said. "Zere is zo much you do not understand. Ze human spirit, it is — a hard tink to kill."

Granny nodded. "Even with a chain saw."

To make her point even clearer, Abigail pinched Wednesday's cheek — *hard*. Wednesday ignored her, continuing to frown at Fester.

If anything, she was now even *more* suspicious.

Later, when all the excitement had died down, Morticia showed Fester up to his unchanged room. The bureau was covered with photographs from when he and Gomez were boys.

There was one of the two of them, very young, next to a crude wooden sign with "Camp Custer" branded into it.

Morticia bent to open Fester's trunk and help him settle in.

"No unpacking — you must be exhausted," she said. "Let me."

"Uh . . . no," Fester said quickly, alarmed by what she might find. "Uh, that's all right . . . you don't have to . . ."

Morticia began removing Fester's burglary equipment from the trunk, stacking it neatly.

"A crowbar," she said. "Dynamite. Cyanide." She laughed gently. "Fester! As if we'd run out."

She patted him on the shoulder, still chuckling. "Good night."

Once she was gone, Fester examined two more photographs in a hand-tooled leather frame on the bureau. Imprinted below the face of the beautiful girl on the left was the name Flora, and below the beautiful girl on the right was the name Fauna. Beautiful identical twins.

Then, the clock struck midnight, and he put the picture down.

It was very late, and it was time for him to get to work. To find the Addams family fortune.

Chapter 8

Trying to be very quiet, Fester opened his bedroom door and peeked out. He saw Wednesday, in her doorway across the hall, staring at him, and quickly ducked back into his room.

"Nosy little brat," he muttered, counted to one hundred, and opened his door again.

This time, Wednesday's door was closed. He looked both ways, then stepped out into the hall to begin his search. By now, everyone else should be asleep — and he certainly didn't want to be disturbed.

He started with the attic, pushing up the trapdoor and climbing inside the dusty old storage room. Seeing a set of glass cases, he headed towards them.

The first case contained a set of mounted butterflies, pinned in place. The second, larger, case held several stuffed vampire bats. The third, and largest, glass case was about three feet high — and empty.

"It's reserved," Wednesday said, suddenly standing behind him, near the trapdoor.

Fester was startled, but tried to act calm. "It's reserved?" he said, as though he were just making conversation. Being friendly to his little niece. "For what?"

Wednesday looked at him with unblinking eyes. "For Skipper."

"For Skipper," Fester repeated uneasily. "Is he . . . a dog?"

"No," Wednesday said. "Skipper isn't a dog." She frowned at him. "That would be cruel."

"Of course," Fester said, gruffly apologetic. "Of course it would be. I'm sorry."

"Skipper is a *bully*," Wednesday said, and blinked. Once.

Unnerved, Fester stared at her, then hurried past her and down through the trapdoor. He ran back to his room and shut the door, leaning up against it, breathing hard.

Once he was sure that Wednesday wasn't following him, he sat on the edge of the bed. A cloud of dust billowed around him. Yawning, he decided to lie down. He sank into the mattress so deeply that he was almost buried alive. Getting comfortable, he burrowed deeper.

Just as he was falling asleep, he heard the excrutiatingly slow creak of his door opening, and sat bolt upright.

"Who's there?" he demanded.

He saw a huge shadow on the wall — a sinister hand with wriggling fingers. He gasped, and lunged for the knife he always kept in his boot, which was on the floor next to his bed.

But, before he could get it, the door slammed shut, and the window exploded open from the force of the raging storm outside, the wet wind snuffing out the candelabra light. There was a bright flash of white lightning, and Fester was horrified to see a hand gripping the bedspread. Crawling towards him. A hand that wasn't his.

One of the candles was still flickering a little, and he seized it, nurturing the flame protectively until it was strong enough to relight the rest of the candles. As the room filled with light, he saw Thing sitting on one of his legs.

Fester jumped with fear, then shook his leg, violently throwing Thing off. But he could still see the disembodied hand on the floor, and so, he screamed.

Screamed *loudly*.

Down the hall, Gomez and Morticia were lying in bed, too happy about Fester's miraculous return to sleep. They heard the scream, and looked even happier.

"My own dear brother," Gomez said, and took a puff on his cigar. "Screams in the night. It can only mean one thing."

They waited in silence, listening. Then, Fester screamed another bloodcurdling scream.

The sound made Morticia smile. "Yes. He's home," she said.

They gazed out through their window at the tor-
rential downpour, and kept smiling as Fester
screamed over and over.

It was so nice to have him back again.

In the morning, Gomez went down to wake up
his brother. He stood there, watching Fester sleep,
with Thing snoozing on his chest like a kitten. It
was one of the sweetest sights he had ever seen.
Gomez gently lifted Thing up, and tucked him into
the pocket of his smoking jacket.

Instantly awake, afraid that Gomez was about to
attack him, Fester leapt from the bed and jumped
on top of his brother, pinning him to the floor. Pulling the knife from his boot, he pressed the blade to
Gomez' throat.

"Ready for breakfast?" Gomez asked cheerfully.
He judo-flipped Fester off his chest, then sprang to
his feet. "It's good to have you back. Let's go!" He
started for the door, then paused, indicating the
knife. "Want to go two out of three?"

Downstairs, the rest of the family was already
eating breakfast in the subterranean kitchen. Once
Gomez and Fester had joined them, only Pugsley
was missing.

As always, the walls were sweating, and smoke
crawled along the floor. Granny worked at the
stove, which was a coal-burning monstrosity with
flames belching out of the oven. The top was a gigantic grill where innards and various unidentifiable

somethings sizzled away. She flipped this offal onto various family member's plates, with Lurch's stolid, steadfast assistance.

Morticia had seated Fester between Gomez and herself, and she had given him their prize pewter place setting with a dragon motif. Only the most honored of guests were allowed to use it.

"May I have the salt?" Wednesday asked.

Morticia lifted the shaker, then stopped. "What do we say?"

"*Now*," Wednesday said dutifully.

Morticia nodded, and passed her the salt.

"What is this?" Fester asked, staring at his plate.

"Mama's *spécialité de la maison*," Morticia said proudly.

Granny looked over from the stove. "Start with the eyes," she said.

Fester shuddered, and pushed his plate away.

"Sleep well?" Morticia asked him.

Fester nodded. "Like the dead."

"Really?" Gomez said, greatly surprised. "Who knew the Bermuda Triangle could change a man so much? You used to toss and turn all night. We had to chain you to the bedposts."

"It doesn't make sense," Wednesday said, her gaze as level as her voice.

Feeling cornered, Fester squirmed in his seat a little. "The Bermuda Triangle is such a large and mysterious place," he said to Wednesday, very condescendingly. "You'd be surprised at all the things you don't know."

"She certainly would," Morticia agreed.

"Wednesday *adores* the Bermuda Triangle. She studies it. Death at sea — she's hooked."

Wednesday gave Fester her least friendly smile. "Ask me *anything*."

Fester hesitated, then turned his back on her to address Gomez. "Being in my old room sure brings back memories," he said. "Remember Camp Custer?"

Gomez' eyes lit up. "For preteen offenders?"

Fester nodded, and they both laughed mischievously.

"Aren't memories precious?" Fester said, guiding the conversation exactly where he wanted it to go. "I'd like to spend today wandering through the house, remembering."

"No, no, no," Gomez said, shaking his head. "Sorry, old man — no wandering today. Today, we're going straight to the vault."

"The *vault*?" Fester said, unable to believe his luck.

"Well, of course," Gomez said, spearing a burned and writhing piece of his breakfast with a fork. "Where else?"

"Where else," Fester agreed, and couldn't help smiling a slow, hideous smile.

Stealing the fortune was going to be much easier than he'd thought.

Chapter 9

They were all still eating when Pugsley came running into the room, dragging a freshly stolen Stop sign, still on its pole. Gomez held up a finger, shushing everyone.

It was quiet for a second, and then they heard the screeching sound of cars heading for a collision. There was more screeching and squealing, then the cars collided with a satisfying crunch of metal.

Everyone at the table beamed.

"Who wants seconds?" Granny asked, then looked at Fester. "Come on," she said with an evil grin. "Don't be shy."

Fester swallowed, hard, and then held out his plate.

After breakfast, Gomez took Fester to the den and the bookcase that was the entrance to the vault. He reached for a book, and Fester was right there with him, his hand on Gomez' hand as he went to pull out the old volume.

"*Greed*," Fester said.

They shared a smile.

The bookcase swung open, and Fester eagerly followed Gomez inside and down into the secret chamber.

"I feel like — we're children again," Gomez said, gleefully running down a flight of steps and into a small circular room. Hundreds of rusty chains were hanging over his head, and he grabbed one, then punched Fester in the shoulder. "Tag — you're it!"

He yanked on the chain, a trapdoor opened, and both of them dropped out of view and onto a long, twisting slide below. Gomez was having a great time; Fester was petrified.

Finally, the slide deposited them on a dock leading to an underground river. Gomez jumped to his feet, full of high spirits, while Fester took his time getting up, very wobbly.

Gomez inhaled deeply, as though they were in a flower-laden meadow. "Smell that air, Fester!"

Fester inhaled — and then gagged.

"Like a tomb!" Gomez said.

Fester nodded, still gagging.

Gomez strode down to the end of the dock, where a rundown, but still magnificent, Venetian gondola was waiting. He jumped aboard, putting on a straw gondolier's hat.

"*Tutto a bordo, fratello mio!*" he said, and gestured to the water. "The sea — your second home."

Fester boarded the gondola gingerly, looking queasy. "Uh — ship ahoy," he said, trying to get into the spirit of things.

Gomez nodded, winding an old Victrola as he

sorted through a pile of 78 rpm records. He found the one he wanted and put it on, singing in a bellowing *basso profundo* as they set sail along the river. He poled the boat along, singing loudly, as Fester hung onto the sides and did his best to smile.

His best wasn't very convincing.

Up in the attic, Wednesday and Pugsley were exploring. They stopped to investigate various grisly items.

"Do you think that's really Uncle Fester?" Pugsley asked.

Wednesday frowned. "Father says so, but I think Mother isn't sure." She stopped in front of an old electric chair. "Pugsley, sit down."

"Why?" Pugsley asked.

"So we can play a game," Wednesday said, guilelessly.

Pugsley shrugged, and climbed into the chair. "What game?"

"It's called . . ." She thought. " 'Is There an Afterlife?' "

Pugsley shrugged. "Okay. Sounds fun."

Still singing, Gomez poled the boat towards a massive metal door, six feet across and ten feet high, set right into the rock of the grotto. He docked at the narrow ledge in front of the door, then jumped out of the boat, with Fester right behind him.

"The, uh, the vault," Fester said, licking his lips in anticipation.

Gomez went to work on the oversized combination lock, giving Fester a knowing smile.

"Two to the right," he said, "ten to the left, and then around to . . . ?"

Fester bit his lip. "Five?" he guessed.

Gomez looked at him, surprised. "*Eleven*," he said. "Two, ten, eleven. Eyes, fingers, toes." He reached for the door handle. "So many years . . . "

"Long, barren years," Fester said, barely able to contain his excitement at the prospect of seeing the great Addams family fortune.

"Years that we wasted," Gomez said sadly.

"Years we'll bring back," Fester assured him, trying to hurry this along.

Gomez nodded. "So we enter together — a triumphant return!"

"We enter as brothers," Fester said, wishing that Gomez would just open the door already. "We enter . . ." Nothing happened. "We enter . . ."

"As one!" Gomez said, and pulled the door open with a dramatic flourish.

Rather than a treasure trove, the vault looked like a decrepit nineteenth-century men's club, with torn red leather chairs and settees, an assortment of torture devices and hunting trophies, and an elaborate bar with a cracked mirror.

"Welcome back!" Gomez said.

Fester was too disappointed to pretend to be enthusiastic. "Thanks."

"Our secret place. *Sanctum sanctorum*." Gomez nudged him. "If these walls could talk, eh, old man?"

"What, uh," Fester looked around, "what would they say?"

Gomez laughed, certain that his brother was joking. "You tell me."

"You go first," Fester said.

Gomez gestured to Fester, out of respect. "No. Senior partner."

"Uh — junior spaceman!" Fester said, gesturing back.

There was a brief silence, then Gomez indicated the bar.

"First, a brandy!" he said. "Do the honors." He bent to open a large wooden box. "I've got a real treat in store."

Fester grumbled his way over to the bar. "Where's the money, you ridiculous imbecile," he muttered. There were six or seven excellent brandies on the well-stocked shelf, and Fester pocketed a sterling silver jigger for a souvenir, then chose a bottle of brandy.

Instantly, the bar spun around, with him on it, revealing — the interior treasure room.

It was everything he had imagined — and more.

Chapter 10

The interior treasure room was a stone cavern, stacked high with gold, jewels, and bizarre but priceless statuary from around the world. It had to be worth *millions*.

Fester had time for one slack-jawed glimpse, and then the bar spun again, returning him to the outer room.

Gomez, who had been too busy digging through the wooden box to notice Fester's carousel ride, stood up with an armload of film cannisters.

"Surprise!" he said, indicating the home movies. "It's showtime!"

Hands shaking — both from the whirl on the bar and the prospect of seeing home movies — Fester poured himself a stiff drink, then replaced the bottle on the shelf.

Up in the attic, Wednesday strapped Pugsley's arms and legs to the electric chair.

"But, if he's not Uncle Fester," Pugsley said, frowning, "then who is he?"

"Somebody else," Wednesday said logically. She pushed a button, and the lights on the chair went on, the entire mechanism humming and vibrating. "It has to warm up," she explained.

"Oh." Pugsley looked down. "Why?"

"So it can kill you," Wednesday said.

"Oh," Pugsley said, looked down, then smiled uncertainly. "I knew that."

Gomez showed home movie after home movie. He and Fester sat side-by-side, in armchairs with the stuffing coming out. As they watched, they smoked cigars and drank brandy from extra-large snifters.

This particular movie was showing the young Gomez and Fester, shark fins strapped to their backs, as they snuck around a corner towards a swimming pool crowded with small children.

Then, there was a jump cut to young Gomez, burying young Fester in the sand at the beach. Fester's head was the only thing showing. A few yards away, a single hand — clearly another person — was struggling to get out of the sand.

Then, the film switched to a formal dance, with Fester and Gomez now in their teens. The Addams boys looked both sinister and dashing in their tuxedos, and Gomez was smoking a cigar.

"Oh, the debutante ball!" Gomez said. "Remember that fateful night?"

"Of course," Fester said, with more confidence than he felt. "Your . . . first cigar."

"What?" Gomez stared at him. "Come on, old

man, I've smoked since I was five. Mother insisted."

On the movie screen, the Addams boys were standing with their dates, the twins from the pictures on Fester's bureau — beautiful redheads with dementia in their eyes.

"Flora and Fauna," Fester said, to cover his tracks. "Quite the pair, eh, Gomez?"

Gomez nodded and sighed, then brought both hands to his chest. "Can you ever forgive me?" he asked.

Fester looked at him blankly. "What?"

"I didn't love them," Gomez said. "Yet, I wooed them, both, out of foolish pride. You were so dashing, you could have had any woman you wanted, dead or alive. And I was so jealous, insanely jealous. I admit that now." He sighed. "But I never meant to drive you off, not to the Bermuda Triangle."

Fester held up a hand, very gracious. "Water under the bridge," he said. "Forgiven. Forgotten."

Gomez held out his arms, and Fester suffered through a big hug. Then, Gomez turned the hug into a painful headlock, and Fester gasped for breath.

"Say it!" Gomez said playfully. "Say the password!"

"The password?" Fester asked, choking. "I . . . I . . ."

Gomez tightened his grip. "Come on, stop fooling. You remember."

"Please," Fester said, his face turning blue. "I'm choking. *Please*."

Gomez, completely perplexed, released him.

"You forgot our secret password?" he said. "The word we used one hundred times a day? Our special private name for each other?"

Fester rubbed his neck. "That was a long time ago," he said, still gasping. "We were children." He scowled at Gomez. "You almost killed me, you demented freak."

Gomez looked at him in shock. "Did you say — demented freak?"

"*Yes*, you demented freak," Fester said.

Gomez' face brightened, and he gave his brother a joyful hug. "Yes!" he said. "Demented freak!"

Up in the attic, the electric chair was really humming. Pugsley was wearing the chair's helmet now, in addition to being strapped down. Wednesday lifted her hand, getting ready to throw the huge master switch.

"But, why would Dr. Pinder-Schloss tell a lie?" Pugsley asked, his voice muffled inside the helmet.

"Because she wants something," Wednesday said, and paused. "Do you have any last requests?"

"Can I have ice cream?" Pugsley asked.

Wednesday thought about that. "No," she said.

Pugsley let out a resigned sigh. "Then just do it."

Just as Wednesday was about to throw the switch, Morticia's head appeared from the trapdoor.

"Children — what are you doing?" she asked, climbing up into the attic.

"I'm going to electrocute him," Wednesday said, sweetly.

"But — we're late for the charity auction," Morticia said.

"Please, Mother, I — " Wednesday started.

Morticia put her hands on her hips, pretending to be very stern. "I said no."

"Please?" Pugsley asked, from under the helmet.

"Oh . . . all right," Morticia said, smiled, and flipped the switch herself.

The high voltage began to sizzle Pugsley. Wednesday watched solemnly, her usual impassive self, and then — that rarest of reactions — she smiled, too.

It was a very special family moment.

Chapter 11

The charity auction was crowded. Margaret Alford stood up on the auction block, holding her hands aloft, still ensnared in the ancient finger trap. And, because she couldn't move her hands and had no choice, she was still wearing the very same clothes she had had on the day before.

On the stage beside her, Judge Womack acted as the event's auctioneer, reading into the microphone from the catalogue.

". . . encrusted with rubies and fifteen emerald chips," he read."It was donated by Morticia and Gomez Addams."

Gomez and Morticia, sitting with their family, looked around, modestly.

People in the crowd looked back, staring at the family with mingled horror and disbelief.

"Remember," Judge Womack said, when nobody made a bid, "the money we raise goes to help the less fortunate. This year, over half our proceeds will benefit the elderly and mentally disabled."

All of the Addamses looked at Granny proudly. She beamed.

"I open the bidding at five thousand dollars," Judge Womack said, to get things started.

"Bah! Not enough!" Gomez thrust up his arm. "Twenty thousand!"

"For the elderly and the insane . . ." Morticia gazed fondly at Granny. "They've *earned* it."

Judge Womack and Margaret were both surprised, and confused, by the bid.

"What are they doing?" Margaret asked in a low voice. "It's theirs."

Judge Womack gave her a warning look.

Out in the audience, Pugsley had a peashooter in his mouth, aimed at Judge Womack. Wednesday glared at him and held out her hand. Sheepishly, he passed her the peashooter.

"I have twenty — " Judge Womack began.

"Twenty-five!" Gomez said, and smiled at Morticia. "*Cara mia.*"

Fester took Morticia's opera glasses and peered appraisingly at the glittering finger trap. His eyes widened, and he kept the glasses, greedily devouring the sight.

"Twenty-five . . ." Judge Womack said.

Morticia raised a bashful hand. "Thirty," she said, and winked at Gomez. "*Mon sauvage.*"

"What are they *doing*?" Margaret whispered.

Judge Womack indicated for her to shut up — immediately.

In the audience, Wednesday now had the peashooter in her mouth, aimed at Judge Womack.

Granny gave her a fierce look, and Wednesday flushed and handed over the peashooter.

Gomez raised his hand. "Thirty-five!"

Morticia raised *her* hand. "Fifty!" she said. She lowered her hand, but kept it extended for Gomez to kiss. Which he did, passionately.

Judge Womack raised his gavel, rather flabbergasted. "I have fifty thousand dollars," he said.

"Your turn, my ecstasy," Morticia said to Gomez.

"It's yours, *amore mio*," he said.

She blushed. "You spoil me . . . *mon amour*."

Judge Womack brought down his gavel. "Sold, to Morticia Addams for fifty thousand dollars!" Then, a projectile hit him in the neck, and he gasped at the stinging pain.

Out in the audience, with the peashooter in her mouth, Granny just smiled.

On the way home, Fester appropriated the finger trap, sitting in the back of the old Duesenberg. He had, immediately, gotten his fingers stuck, and he stared at the jewels, as though hypnotized.

Morticia, sitting beside him, also admired the trap. "Isn't it enchanting?" she said. "Gomez, you shouldn't have done it. So much money."

Gomez shrugged. "It's for charity. And it belongs with the family."

Fester pulled his fingers, trying to free them. "How do you take it off?"

Morticia released the trap. "There's a trick to it," she said. "*Of course*."

Gomez glanced at Wednesday, then leaned forward from his place on the other side of Morticia and, eyebrows knitted, frowned at Fester.

Maybe his long-lost brother's sudden appearance *was* too good to be true.

After they got home, Gomez sat down in the dining room, his huge model train layout filling the room. He watched as the Lionel train raced through the remains of a strip-mined mountain terrace.

Thing galloped into view from around one of the mountains, then paced back and forth in front of Gomez' transformers.

" *'How do you take it off?'* " Gomez said to Thing, still very upset. "That's absurd! The finger trap was a party favor at his tenth birthday!"

Demonically, he started his second train, setting it on a sure collision course with the first.

Upstairs, Fester, with cool professionalism, slipped his safecracking tools into the bandoliers strapped across his chest, and prepared to go to the vault.

He reached into his top dresser drawer for the nitroglycerin, and came up with the photo of young Fester and Gomez being brought home from Camp Custer by the UPS man. He stared at the picture, then tossed it aside as if it had burned him.

He picked up the nitroglycerin, and went back to his preparations.

In the dining room, puffing black smoke, the model trains raced towards one another, towards the inevitable. His emotions churning like the locomotive wheels, Gomez ranted and raved to Thing.

"He wore that finger trap for two years!" Gomez said. "Mother had to teach him to eat with his feet! And the combination, and the password, and my cigar — and he slept so well!"

Like Gomez, Thing paced furiously.

Something was very, very wrong.

Chapter 12

Granny sat in the kitchen, reading cookbooks, the noise of the train set so loud that it was hard to concentrate. But . . . cooking was her *life*.

She was consulting two different books at once: *The Joy of Cooking* and *Gray's Anatomy*. The combination was wonderful, and deadly.

A piercing train whistle resounded through the house, shaking the kitchen table, and Granny frowned, leaning one elbow on each book so she would still be able to read.

So many recipes, so little time.

Up in Pugsley's room, Morticia was seated on the bed with a family photo album on her lap. Wednesday and Pugsley, in their pajamas, sat on either side of her, looking at the pictures.

Pugsley pointed at one. "Is that Father, when he was little?"

"Yes." Morticia pointed at another figure in the picture. "And that's Uncle Fester."

Wednesday frowned at the chaotic black-and-white-scene. "Where are they?"

"At a birthday party." Morticia pointed. "See the fire trucks?"

From the dining room, they could hear Gomez' voice howling "All aboard!" followed by another whistle blast.

Morticia looked very worried. "Oh, no," she said.

"Father's playing with his trains," Pugsley said nervously.

Wednesday nodded, looking up at her mother with a very concerned expression. "He must be upset," she said.

"It's always a bad sign," Morticia agreed, grimly. "*Hobbies*."

Down in the den, Fester removed the well-worn copy of *Greed* from the shelf, and the secret panel opened.

He was on his way to the vault.

In the dining room, the model trains whistled at full blast, shrieking in warning as they rounded Dead Man's Curve, heading for each other. Inside one of the trains, a little passenger looked out fearfully.

Gomez was still pacing around in a fury.

"These thoughts!" he shouted. "I'm in torment! What is truth? What is fiction?"

Thing pounded the table in frustration, equally upset.

* * *

Lurch was up in his bedroom, in his too-small bed, wearing his nightshirt and cap, carefully sewing a button on a shirt.

The chug of the trains was now shaking the entire house. Lurch's needle slipped when he heard one especially loud whistle, and he pricked his finger. He automatically put it in his mouth, and looked down in the general direction of the dining room, where Gomez was still raving.

When a member of the Addams family was upset, Lurch was upset, too.

Fester made his way to the small circular room where the secret chamber was. He pushed against the wall, wondering if that would make it open. Then, he remembered what Gomez had done, and looked up at the chains hanging from the ceiling, each with a rusted metal grip on the end.

The question was, which one should he pull?

Randomly, he yanked one, and the chain yanked back, pulling him straight up into the air. With a screech of pulleys and gears, the chain rocketed him, while he hung on for dear life, towards a narrow gap in what might or might not have been a ceiling.

Fester closed his eyes — and disappeared into the gap.

Morticia and the children listened to the whistling, chugging cacophony of the trains.

"He's using the diesel," Pugsley whispered.

There was a shrill blast.

"The covered bridge," Wednesday said softly.

There was another blast, and Morticia looked very concerned.

"Dead Man's Curve," she said.

Wednesday tugged on her sleeve. "I know what he's worried about."

"So do I, darling," Morticia said, trying to hide her anxiety. "But let's get to bed. Now, have you brushed your teeth and washed behind your ears?"

Pugsley hung his head. "I did," he said. "I'm sorry."

There was another blast from the trains.

"Is that man really Uncle Fester?" Wednesday asked.

Morticia was about to answer her when she saw Fester zooming through the floor-to-ceiling fish tank. She glanced quickly at the children, to make sure that they hadn't noticed.

"Time for bed," she said, standing up.

Wednesday and Pugsley protested, but not much. So Morticia tucked them in and headed downstairs.

She had something very important to do.

The train crash was imminent, and Gomez fell to his knees on the floor.

"Spirits above me — give me a sign!" he shouted.

The trains collided with a great crash and rending of metal, smoke and flames bursting out all over the place.

As signs went, it wasn't a very positive one.

* * *

Out in the yard, a coal chute set in the side of the house opened up, dropping the soaked, disoriented Fester unceremoniously to the ground at Morticia's feet.

Silhouetted by the full moon, she stood regally above him, her velvet cloak covering her night clothes.

"Sleepless night?" she asked, pointedly. "Walk with me, Fester."

She turned, gliding away across the yard, giving Fester no choice but to follow her.

They were going to the cemetery.

Chapter 13

It was a chilly night . . . and it was even colder in the cemetery. Morticia led Fester along a path that wound among the ornate tombstones of the Addams dead. Gomez' golf balls were everywhere — on the ground, in statues' upturned hands, in their open mouths.

As they passed them, Morticia pointed out various monuments. The marble statues looked so real that they could be alive.

"Aunt LaBorgia," she said, indicating one. "Executed by a firing squad. Cousin Fledge — torn limb from limb by four wild horses. And darling Uncle Eimar . . ."

Uncle Eimar was a hooded executioner with an upraised ax. There was an unearthly moan, which seemed to come from the tomb. Fester flinched; Morticia didn't.

"Buried alive," she said. "Psychopaths, fiends, mad-dog killers — *roots*, Fester. Lest we forget."

Among the statuary was a marble vulture, posed with the dignity of an eagle on a flagpole, but the flagpole was actually a replica of Fester's bald head.

"Your beloved Muerto," Morticia said. "After you left, he was simply . . . a different vulture." She sighed. "He wouldn't circle. He wouldn't peck. *That's* how much you mean to this family."

Fester didn't say anything.

They reached the mausoleum, where Mother and Father Addams were. It stood on a knoll, the highest point in the cemetery. Poison ivy covered the dilapidated Greco-Roman tomb. Mother and Father Addams had been depicted as a god and goddess, with charioteers driving their steeds to the netherworld. Naturally, Father Addams was smoking the ubiquitous Addams cigar.

Morticia gazed up at the likenesses of Mother and Father Addams, but Fester averted his eyes. Somehow, the faces seemed to be staring directly at *him*.

"Mother and Father Addams," Morticia said wistfully. "Imagine what we owe them. Oh, Fester, how I wish the children could have known them better. But tell that to an angry mob."

She turned to trace the family crest, carved into the mausoleum. The top of the crest was a vulture, and the background was composed of three lions' heads. In one panel, a huntsman held open the lion's jaws; in the next, the lion had swallowed him up to his torso; in the last panel, the lion had swallowed

69

the huntsman completely but for one dangling foot. On a banner at the bottom was the family motto, in Latin.

"Three lions rampant," Morticia said, very thoughtfully. "The vulture ascendant. And our credo: *'Sic gorgiamus allos subjectatos nunc.'* 'We gladly feast on those who would subdue us.' " She paused, for reflection. "Not just pretty words. As an Addams, you understand completely — *don't you?*"

Fester coughed. "As an Addams, yes, I do," he said.

Morticia looked at him for a long minute.

"Good night, Fester," she said, and headed for the house. Then, she turned. "Rest in peace."

With that, she was gone.

In the morning, Fester called Abigail. He was hunched over the phone in the hallway, his eyes darting to make sure no one was around to overhear.

"They're on to me, Mother!" he said frantically. "I'm almost sure! . . . Of course, I've tried. I still can't find it. . . . You've got to come over here."

Down the hall, Wednesday was bound and gagged on a chair. Pugsley ran up to Fester, holding two bottles of poison. Somewhat distracted, Fester pointed to one. Pugsley nodded, and ran off.

"Don't say that," Fester said into the phone. "Mother, you *know* that I do, come on. . . ."

* * *

In the kitchen, Granny and Lurch were doing the dishes. Granny would rinse, Lurch would dry, and then hand each dish to Thing, who stacked them.

Morticia sat at the kitchen table, sipping her morning cup of tea. Wednesday, freed from her ropes, stood in front of her, holding up a large, nasty-looking carving knife.

"Is that for your brother?" Morticia asked.

Wednesday nodded.

Morticia took the knife away from her. "No, I don't think so," she said, then handed Wednesday a much larger, even nastier-looking knife.

Wednesday took the knife, and ran out of the room.

Morticia watched her go, then sighed. "His trains are everywhere, the children are beside themselves — this can't go on," she said. "How can I help him? Tell me, Mama."

"Well, let's look it up." Granny wiped her hands and opened a large, ragged leatherbound book, thumbing through the pages. "Troubled husbands, troubled husbands . . . adultery . . ."

Morticia shook her head. "Oh, no."

Granny kept looking. "Financial, money troubles . . ."

"No," Morticia said.

Granny looked some more. "Turned into a toad or reptile . . ."

"Is there an index?" Morticia asked, getting a little impatient.

"Ah! Here it is," Granny said trimphantly. "Suspicion and anxiety, in husbands."

Morticia leaned to read over her shoulder, very eager. "What does it say?"

"Drain all his blood, replace it with vinegar overnight," Granny read aloud. "Leave a headless rooster beneath his pillow. Smear his forehead, palms, and feet with the tears of a stillborn monkey. Add milk."

"I can't do that," Morticia said, offended. "It's barbaric. Really, Mama. I'm surprised at you." She sniffed disdainfully. "*Milk*."

Lurch growled in agreement.

Abigail had come over at once, and now she and Fester were up in his room. Fester was sitting on the bed, kneading his hands, very upset. Abigail was inspecting the room, quite appalled by what she saw.

"They know I'm a fraud," Fester said. "The whole bunch. It's not going to work!"

"*Who* knows?" Abigail asked. "Gomez, that overheated moron?"

Fester shook his head. "He's no moron! He's Fester's brother. They had some awful fight, years ago. He's suspicious. They all are — I can tell."

"Well, it's a good thing I came over," she said. "I can counsel the troubled family. Ease their distress. It's my calling. Remember, Gordon . . ."

"What?" Fester asked sulkily.

Abigail smiled. "I'm a doctor."

And, a few minutes later, she was sitting in the drawing room with Gomez and Morticia.

"Dr. Pinder-Schloss is here to help," Morticia

said to Gomez, then looked at Abigail. "Should Gomez speak with Fester? He's right outside the door."

"I *would* speak with Fester," Gomez said, and got up, stalking towards the door, "if that *were* Fester, but that's not!" He glared at the closed door. "That's an imposter!" he yelled. "An imposter!"

Chapter 14

On the other side of the door, Fester glared back, then stormed away. He was marching towards his room, when he heard Wednesday and Pugsley playing.

"O villain, villain, smiling, damned villain!" Wednesday was saying, down in the front hall.

"Who calls me a villain?" Pugsley yelled boldly. "Breaks my pate across? Plucks off my beard and blows it in my face?"

"If I must strike you dead, I will!" Wednesday vowed.

Fester got a genuine gleam in his eye. "Bloodshed!" he said.

He hurried to the top of the staircase, and saw Wednesday and Pugsley with swords drawn, dueling. They thrust and parried, hacked and sliced. Then, Puglsey ran Wednesday through. She staggered and fell down dead.

"No! No!" Fester ran downstairs. "Give me that sword."

Pugsley handed him his sword.

"Haven't you ever slaughtered anyone?" Fester asked.

Wednesday opened her eyes, still on the floor. "He's *only* a child," she said.

"No excuse." Fester pointed the sword at Wednesday's throat. "Aim for a major artery. The jugular."

Wednesday nodded, the sword at her throat. "That's what *I* said."

In the drawing room, Gomez was still full of sound and fury.

"A faker! A phony!" he proclaimed. "An utter fraud! A base, deceitful — "

Abigail cut him off. "Mr. Addams, I beleef I am understandink you," she said. "I vill help. Jais? Ze theory of displacement — is zis familiar?"

"No," Gomez said, but he liked the sound of it. "Have you, Tish?"

Morticia shook her head.

"Ha!" Abigail said. "It is too excitink. I vill explain."

"Is it unpleasant?" Gomez asked, hopefully.

"Deeply," Abigail said.

Gomez sat down beside Morticia, taking her hand. They were both fascinated.

"Your very own bruzzer — you drive him avay," Abigail said. "Go! Off viz you! But zen, you are feelink ze little black monster."

Gomez frowned. "Pugsley?"

"*Guilt*," Abigail said, and nodded several times. "Jais! Your bruzzer returns, you feel guilty — you *displace*."

"I do?" Gomez asked.

Morticia was convinced — and impressed. "Of course," she said, nodding.

"Ze feelinks in your brain cells, zey bubble and zey collide," Abigail explained. "You suspect tinks. You luff him, but you resent him. Luff, hate, hate, luff. Like for Mama, no?"

"But" — Gomez looked confused — "I didn't hate my mother. It was an accident."

"Is very common psychosis," Abigail said. "I am seeink it every day."

"Lucky doctor," Morticia said, her expression just a bit envious.

"Displacement!" Gomez tried the word out for himself. "How bizarre. And here, I imagined Fester was the problem. He's sullen . . ."

"He's furtive . . ." Morticia agreed.

Gomez nodded, excitedly. "He's back-stabbing . . ."

"He sulks . . ." Morticia said.

"I suspect him," Gomez admitted.

"You're unbalanced," Morticia said.

"And" — Gomez glanced at her doubtfully — "I hate him . . ."

"But that's love!" Morticia said.

Gomez jumped to his feet. "You're right! He *is* Fester!"

Delighted to see her husband back to his old self,

Morticia smiled at Abigail. "Thank you, Dr. Pinder-Schloss."

Abigail's shrug was self-deprecating. "I do vat I can," she said.

Up in Wednesday's room, Fester was sitting on a leather couch, with Pugsley and Wednesday snuggled up on either side. They were all looking at an enormous, ancient book open on Fester's lap. The title was *Wounds, Scars, and Gouges.*

"You see, children?" Fester said. "There's a lot to learn." He turned the page. "*Gangrene.*"

Pugsley looked up at him with admiration. "Uncle Fester, how do you know so much?"

Fester shrugged. "I've been around. I pick things up."

"In the Bermuda Triangle?" Wednesday asked, still suspicious.

Fester ignored her, turning another page. "Look, children — a new chapter!"

"Oh, boy!" Pugsley said.

They all stared at the chapter heading, enthralled.

"*Scabs,*" they said together.

It was later, and an explosion ripped through the backyard, dirt and debris flying everywhere. As the smoke cleared, Fester was still crouched over a detonator. Wednesday and Pugsley were right next to him.

"See?" Fester said, indicating the rubble-filled

yard. "It's perfect for small homes, carports, and toolsheds."

"What about picnics?" Wednesday asked.

Fester smiled at her approvingly. Then, he reached into a crate, pulling out a hand grenade. The children's eyes sparkled, as though it were Christmas Day.

Up above them, Abigail stood at the window of Fester's room. She looked out, watching him play with the children, her expression very displeased.

She did not like what she was seeing.

Chapter 15

When Fester came back upstairs, Abigail was waiting for him.

"Everyone will be at the children's play tonight, correct?" she said stiffly.

"Oh, yes." Fester grinned at her. "I've been working with them. It's going to be fun!"

"Fun? *Fun?*" Abigail said, absolutely livid. "Is that what we're here for? *Fun?*" She slapped him across the face, then grabbed him and hugged him. "Darling, I'm sorry! You see what they've driven me to? I've raised a hand to my child, my reason to live." She gave her head a brisk shake to clear it. "Anyway. It's very simple. You can't go to the play."

Fester's face fell. "But . . . the kids . . ."

"The house will be deserted," Abigail reminded him. "The vault will be ours!"

"But — " Fester began.

Abigail hugged him to her. "Soon we'll have the money, and we'll be far from here," she said. "Loving mother, grateful son. . . . This is no time for theater." She gave his head a twist, tightening the hug. *"Understood?"*

Fester nodded reluctantly.

That night, when everyone else was getting ready to go to the play, Fester stood alone on the roof, looking out over the cemetery, brooding.

"There you are!" Gomez said from the door, and came over to join him at the railing. He smiled at his brother. "What a fool I was to doubt you," he said. "Dr. Pinder-Schloss explained everything. Displacement — it's a common psychosis. Isn't that grand?"

Fester sighed. "Is it?"

Gomez threw a friendly arm around Fester's shoulders. "Look at it, Fester," he said, gazing down into the cemetery, morbid and magnificent in the moonlight. "The primeval ooze. Quicksand. Fumes. Toxic waste. And — it's all ours, Fester. You *belong* here, old man."

Fester shook his head unhappily. "You don't know what you're asking. You have a beautiful wife. Wonderful kids." He gestured towards the swamp. "A wasteland. I'm . . . in the way."

"In the way?" Gomez said. "A brother?"

Fester nodded. "For you, Gomez, life is all fun and games. A dance in the graveyard. Stench and decay. But," he sighed again, "things change."

"Precisely!" Gomez said. "You're back! Those years apart, Fester, we can't do that again."

Fester shrugged, unhappily.

"You're *home*," Gomez said, and held out his

hand. Thing put a golf club in it. Gomez passed the club to Fester, and Thing supplied him with another for himself.

"Fore!" Gomez yelled, and swung his club.

The two men hit golf balls off the roof, and over the cemetery, into the darkness. Far off, in the distance, there was the sound of a window breaking.

After the brief diversion of hitting golf balls, Fester went back to his room and sat on the edge of the bed to brood there, instead of the roof.

Wednesday and Pugsley appeared in the doorway.

"Come on, Uncle Fester," Pugsley said. "Come to the play."

Fester glared at him. "I said I was busy!"

Wednesday looked even more unhappy than usual. "But, you said you'd help us," she said. "With the Shakespeare. And the pus."

"I changed my mind!" Fester said, and slouched forward, putting his head in his hands.

The family Duesenberg pulled up in front of the school building. Bystanders paused to eye the strange and wondrous automobile. Lurch stepped out of the car and opened the rear door with great ceremony.

As the bystanders gaped, the Addams family stepped out of the car, looking as though they had just arrived at the Academy Awards. The crowd moved aside to let them pass.

Inside, the lobby was packed with the families

of students. A wholesome and overeager young woman detached herself from a group of teachers and approached Morticia.

"Mrs. Addams?" she said. "May I see you for a moment? I'm Susan Firkins, Wednesday's teacher."

"Oh, of course, Mrs. Firkins," Morticia said, nodding. "Wednesday's told us so much about you." She looked at her sympathetically. "Have you ever heard from your husband?"

Mrs. Firkins' eyes widened, but then she just took Morticia's arm and led her over to a bulletin board hanging on one side of the lobby.

"Wednesday is an excellent student," she said, "but frankly, I'm concerned. This is our class bulletin board and, this month, our theme is 'Our Heroes.' People we love and admire."

Morticia nodded pleasantly.

"You see, Susan Ringo has chosen the President." Mrs. Firkins pointed to a magazine cover of President Bush, hanging next to a child's essay. "Isn't that sweet? And Harmony Feld has picked Diane Sawyer." She indicated a photo of Diane Sawyer, hanging next to Harmony's essay.

"Have you spoken to her parents?" Morticia asked, very concerned.

Mrs. Firkins looked at her with complete incomprehension. "Uh, anyway," she said. "Wednesday brought in this picture — Calpurnia Addams." She showed Morticia an oil painting of an evil-looking crone.

Morticia was touched by this. "Wednesday's

great-aunt Calpurnia," she said, very proud. "She was burned as a witch in 1706. They said she danced naked in the town square, and enslaved a minister."

Mrs. Firkins stared at her, shocked. "Really?"

"Oh, yes," Morticia said. "But don't worry, we've told Wednesday — college first."

Mrs. Firkins just stared.

When Morticia went back to the rest of the family, Tully and Margaret were chatting with Gomez. Their son, Tully, Jr., was wearing a felt elf costume.

"Isn't he adorable?" Margaret asked, her hands on his shoulders. "I made this myself."

"It's charming," Morticia said, and patted him on the head. "What is he — a lizard?"

"An *elf*." Margaret knelt down, wiping her son's face with a Kleenex. "Look at you — that's better. You are just *too precious* for words. Why, I could just eat you alive!"

"No, Margaret," Morticia said, frowning. "Too young."

There was a brief silence.

"So, Gomez," Tully said. "Um, where's Fester this evening?"

Gomez shrugged. "Moody — as usual. We're all out on a jaunt, and he's home alone, in that big empty house."

"What a shame," Tully said, his eyes gleaming.

Granny and Lurch walked by, hawking one of Granny's delicacies to the crowd.

"Toad on a stick!" Granny said. "Get your red-hot toad on a stick! Can't enjoy the show without your toad on a stick!"

Back at the house, Fester was sitting at his desk, working with great concentration. It would appear that he was building a bomb. He glanced at the clock, frowned, and started working more quickly.

Chapter 16

When he saw Judge Womack across the school lobby, Gomez went over to him, wanting to be a good neighbor.

"I was hoping you'd come over one day and play a round of golf," he said. "Not to brag, but I've got a beautiful little nine-hole pitch-and-putt set up in my cemetery."

Judge Womack tossed his head and turned away. "Never."

"Ahh," Gomez said. "A previous engagement." He tucked one of his cigars in Judge Womack's breast pocket, and went back to join his family.

The show was very long and, so far, the Addams family wasn't enjoying it much. They sat, watching half a dozen adorable seven year olds up on the stage, singing, "Getting to Know You." The children finished, to the enthusiastic applause of an auditorium full of parents.

Morticia and Gomez politely joined in, while

Lurch fidgeted, and Granny slumped, bored, in her chair.

"The children are next," Morticia said.

Lurch stopped fidgeting, and Granny straightened up.

Backstage, Wednesday and Pugsley sat at the makeup mirror, putting on their armor. Fester was suddenly behind them, reflected in the mirror.

"I changed my mind," he said gruffly and thrust a package towards them.

Over at the Addamses' mansion, Abigail was hammering on the door with the knocker.

"Gordon?" she called sweetly. "Oh, Gordon?"

There was no answer.

"Where are you!" She pounded on the door. "I never should have used him!"

She clomped down the porch steps and headed around the side of the house, peering in windows, trying to find a way in.

In the school auditorium, Fester pushed people aside, forcing his way to where his family was seated. They were very pleased to see him.

"I knew you couldn't stay away, old man," Gomez whispered, then sat back to enjoy the show.

Over at the house, standing on tiptoe, Abigail tried yet another window.

Below her, vines came snaking out and wrapped themselves firmly around her ankles. She stared down at them, then screamed as the vines went taut, preparing to pull her into the house.

She screamed again, but there was no one to hear her, and no escape.

Pugsley and Wednesday were doing beautifully, up on the stage. Wearing elaborate costumes, they dueled their way to the climax of their scene from *Hamlet*, acting their little Addamses' hearts out.

"How all occasions do inform against me, and spur my dull revenge!" Wednesday cried. "O, from this time forth, my thoughts be bloody or be nothing worth! If I must strike you dead, I will!"

Pugsley landed the first blow, slashing Wednesday's arm. Her sleeve tore, and blood spurted.

"A hit!" he said. "A very palpable hit!"

They pressed the attack, drawing more blood. In a fatal blow, Pugsley sliced open Wednesday's jugular. She made horrible noises as the blood spurted in arterial squirts.

"Oh, proud death!" she gasped. "What feast is toward in thine eternal cell?"

In a final, vengeful moment, she hacked at Pugsley's loft arm, cutting it off, sending a gusher of blood out of his stump. The arm dropped to the stage and bounced off, landing in Judge Womack's lap.

Onstage, Wednesday clutched her bleeding throat.

"Sweet oblivion, open your arms," she said weakly, and fell dead.

The audience sat perfectly still, jaws agape, deep in shock.

Then, the Addams family leapt as one to their feet, applauding wildly.

"Bravo!" Gomez shouted. "Author! Author!"

The stage lights came up, and Pugsley and Wednesday bowed deeply, accepting their family's applause.

Fester clapped louder than anybody.

Later that night, Fester tucked Wednesday into bed. The two of them were now devoted friends.

". . . and there were sailors, and pirates, and an airplane full of tourists," he said, in the middle of a story. "All lost in the Triangle."

Wednesday clasped her hands together, thrilled. "Uncle Fester, someday will you take me there?" she asked.

He nodded. "It's a promise. Good night, Wednesday. You were terrific."

He kissed her on the forehead. She held out her headless doll, and Fester kissed the doll's empty neck. Then, Wednesday held out the doll's severed head.

Fester smiled, and kissed it, too.

Out in the cemetery, Morticia stood in the moonlight, while Gomez sat on a bench nearby.

"What a sublime evening," Morticia said. "A theatrical triumph!"

"A Shakespearean delight!" Gomez agreed. "All hail Fester!"

"It's like a dream," Morticia said, gazing around the cemetery. "When we first met, years ago, it was an evening much like this. Magic in the air. A boy . . ."

Gomez nodded. "A girl . . ."

"An open grave . . ." Morticia said nostalgically, and sat down beside him. "It was my first funeral."

Gomez put his arm around her. "You were so beautiful — pale and mysterious," he said. "No one even *looked* at the corpse."

"Your cousin, Balthazar," Morticia said, and then smiled at him. "You were still a suspect. I couldn't stop staring, all during the eulogy. Your eyes. Your moustache. Your laugh."

"You bewitched me," Gomez said, his eyes aglow with romance. "I proposed that very night."

"Just think," Morticia said, looking at the tombstones. "Someday, *we'll* be buried here. Side by side, six feet under. In matching coffins. Our lifeless bodies, rotting together, for all eternity."

"*Cara mia!*" Gomez said, aroused by all of this.

"*Mon sauvage!*" Morticia said passionately.

They embraced in the moonlight.

Bright and early the next morning, Lurch was in the conservatory, sweeping. Among the plants, he came upon Abigail, tightly wrapped in a plant cocoon.

He growled.

She was not a very pretty sight.

Chapter 17

In the kitchen, a cheerful Addams breakfast was underway.

"Did you like the blood?" Pugsley asked Fester.

"Perfect," Fester said. "A full bucket. I was so proud."

"Weren't we all," Morticia said. "Wednesday, play with your food."

There was something moving in Wednesday's cereal bowl and, obediently, she teased it with her fork.

Over at the sideboard, Granny screamed, and everyone looked up.

"Mama?" Morticia asked, worried.

Granny pulled the bones of a shin and foot out of one of the serving dishes.

"Who put this in here?" she demanded.

Pugsley and Fester exchanged a conspiratorial glance and giggle.

Granny frowned at them, her hands on her hips. "That's for *company*," she said.

Gomez shook his head, amused. "Rascals," he said, and gave Pugsley a chip-off-the-old-block pat on the head.

Abigail came in, peeling off bits of the vines that had encased her.

"Doctor!" Gomez said, delighted to see her. "You were so right! What an evening!"

"Fester fit right in," Morticia said, happily.

Gomez nodded. "The displacement is over!"

Abigail glared at Fester. "Vell, isn't zat . . . nice," she said.

"Does he really have to go?" Wednesday asked, reaching out to take her uncle's hand.

"Jais," Abigail said, very grim. "He does."

The table got very quiet.

"Well." Gomez broke the silence. "If he insists upon leaving, we shall mark the occasion. Tish?"

Morticia turned to Fester. "We've planned a farewell party," she said.

Gomez nodded. "We've invited the whole clan."

Amazed by the gesture, Fester smiled tremulously.

"Vat a luffly gesture," Abigail said, and looked daggers at Fester.

"Bloodshed . . . anguish . . . breakfast . . ." Morticia said, and let out a contented sigh. "We're a family again. And we owe it all to you, Dr. Pinder-Schloss."

"Please," Abigail said, forcing a smile. "Greta."

Morticia smiled back. "Greta."

Abruptly, Abigail stood up, snapping her fingers.

"Fester," she said. "Valk me out."

Fester looked sadly at his unfinished breakfast, then followed her out of the room.

"Well?" Abigail said, as they walked outside.

"I'm fine, Mother," Fester assured her. "I'm completely in control."

Abigail stopped and grabbed him by both arms, giving him a shake.

"They're not your family, Gordon," she said. "I am. They don't love you. I do. They're evil and corrupt and degraded. I can *give* you that."

"I'm fine," Fester said, and looked longingly back at the house. "Really."

She frowned at him. "We'll see."

They got to the end of the front walk, and Gate. "Open up!" Abigail bellowed.

Even Gate was intimidated by that — and swung open.

That night, Morticia went to the conservatory, pleased to find Fester cutting the blooms from her roses.

"We're opening the ballroom now," she said.

Fester hesitated, but put down his scissors and went with her.

In the hallway outside the ballroom, each member of the family was given a lighted candelabra to hold as they stood in front of the tall, oaken double doors.

Gomez unlatched them and then, together, they all pushed the doors open.

Moonlight streamed in through the floor-to-ceiling windows, revealing the true enormity of the ballroom. It was like something out of a rococo palace. There was a lofty domed ceiling, decorated with figures worthy of Dante. The black marble floors glistened, and the furniture and banquet tables were funereally shrouded. Like some primeval sea, the shrouds undulated in the breeze that came in through the open door.

Gomez stepped up to Morticia, embraced her, and they began to dance.

Fester remained frozen in the center of the ballroom, overwhelmed by the grandeur.

"A party," he said softly. "For *me* . . ."

Gomez and Morticia waltzed past him.

"All for you!" Morticia said, and let Gomez whirl her away.

"Tish — how long has it been since we've waltzed?" he asked.

"Oh, Gomez," Morticia said ruefully. "*Hours.*"

The guest began to arrive and soon the party was in full swing. Gomez and Morticia were resplendent in their party clothes, Morticia wearing a formal version of her black sheath, and Gomez in black velvet lounging pajamas, smoking jacket, and fez.

A small orchestra played a fractured waltz, with Thing serving as a third hand on the bass. Gomez and Morticia danced among the Addams family relations — the portrait gallery of grotesques come to life.

Dexter and Donald Addams, the two-headed cousin, was there, wearing matching turtlenecks. Cousin Ophelia Addams, looking like a Tennessee Williams heroine who had just been fished out of the Mississippi, had come. Slosh Addams, who was living proof that a man could look *just like* a toad, and *still* make a killing on Wall Street, had come, and brought his lovely, child-sized wife, Lois.

Also dancing were Digit Addams, his four arms holding his date, an overaged Heidi with thick blonde braids, and Cousin Lumpy Addams, a teenage hunchback in a loud blazer, who was dancing by himself.

Dexter and Donald danced Ophelia over to Gomez and Morticia.

"I wonder — I wonder — " they said, echoing each other " — what happened — what happened — to Fester — to Fester."

"Still primping, I suppose," Gomez said.

Ophelia, waterlogged and bleary-eyed, gave Morticia a spacey Thorazine smile. "Where is Fester?" she asked.

"Soon, Ophelia," Morticia said kindly. "Soon."

Ophelia tilted her head, and looked at Morticia vaguely. "Where am *I*?" she asked.

Hearing a car, Lurch opened the front door to greet the newest guest. When he saw who it was, his face lit up.

Cousin It had arrived.

Chapter 18

After parking his bubble-topped It-mobile, Cousin It flipped up the top and climbed out. Cousin It was a hairball in a homburg, who gleeped and squeaked in a language that the Addams family had no trouble understanding.

Lurch was delighted to escort him inside. Gomez and Morticia came over instantly to greet him.

"It, old man!" Gomez said cheerfully.

"*Bleep gibber, ooot, ooot*," Cousin It said.

Morticia nodded. "You're right. *Far* too long."

Cousin It looked around, obviously checking out the women. He saw Margaret on the dance floor with Tully.

"*Ooot gibber bleep*," Cousin It said to Gomez and Morticia, excusing himself, then he ran a hand through his hair, slicking it back — and made a bee-line for Margaret.

Throughout the party, Margaret had been clinging stiffly to Tully, trying to ignore all of the Addamses' weirdness.

"The first time we've been dancing in ages," she

complained, "and you take me *here*."

"It's a formal occasion," Tully said defensively.

"Just don't let me out of your sight," Margaret said, hanging on.

There was a tap on her shoulder, and she turned. Before her was Cousin It, hat in hand, eager to cut in.

"*Oot, ooot, ooot*," Cousin It said, took her in his arms, and spun away with her.

Up in Fester's bathroom, Abigail was shaving Fester's head to ensure that he would still be completely bald. She was using scalding hot water and a straight razor, and the room was filled with steam.

"You'll make your appearance," she said. "then slip away from the party."

"How?" Fester asked. "I'm the guest of honor."

"Just *do* it," Abigail said.

Downstairs, Wednesday was dancing with Lumpy Addams, the teenage hunchback.

"Wednesday?" Morticia asked, coming over.

Always polite, Wednesday stopped dancing. "Yes, Mother?"

"Could you run upstairs and check on your uncle?" Morticia asked.

Wednesday nodded, running off.

"Thank you, darling." Morticia turned to look at Lumpy. "Why, Lumpy Addams. Look at you. All grown up."

Lumpy hunched more, bashfully.

* * *

Wednesday knocked on Fester's door, and when he didn't answer, she opened it.

"Uncle Fester?" she called, hearing water running in his bathroom, the sound of voices beneath it.

Then, the water stopped with a final clang of the pipes, and she could hear the voices clearly.

"Yes, Mother, I understand," Fester was saying. "I hear you."

"I hope so, Gordon," Abigail said. "I'm counting on you. Don't buckle."

Gordon? Wednesday's eyes got huge as she listened.

"It's not going to be easy," Fester said, inside the bathroom. "There are people everywhere."

"You can do it, if you just stop whining," Abigail said. "No one likes that — it's unattractive."

"All right, fine," Fester said. "I *will* try and reach the vault tonight. But, if I can't, well — " He hesitated. "Then, that's it. Okay, Mother?"

Wednesday threw open the bathroom door.

"You *are* a fake!" she said. "I knew it!"

Abigail and Fester whirled around to face her. The straight razor in Abigail's hand caught the light, glinting menacingly.

"Come here, little vun," Abigail said, her voice oozing charm. "Ve von't hurt you."

Fester just stood there, visibly torn by which side to take.

"Wednesday, I — " he began.

Abigail's pleasant façade disintegrated. "Get her!" she said, and shoved him towards Wednesday.

Afraid now, Wednesday ran out of his room, and into her own room, slamming the door behind her.

Galvanized by the hold his mother still had on him, Fester went after her and kicked the door open just in time to see Wednesday throw open a trap-door in the floor and disappear down it.

Fester tried to find the door, but the edges were seamless. He felt the boards, fruitlessly, then pounded the floor in frustration.

Outside, next to the coal chutes, there were two smaller chutes — one marked "Pugsley," and one marked "Wednesday." Wednesday slid out of her chute, and hit the ground running.

She ran as fast as she could, into the cemetery, and the darkness of the night.

Lurch escorted two more guests, Flora and Fauna Amor — the twins from the home movies — into the ballroom. He took their wraps, revealing that they were, in fact, a pair of Siamese twins. Twenty-five years later, they still looked quite beautiful, and quite mad.

Gomez approached, shielding his eyes. "Flora and Fauna Amor! I cannot see! I'm blinded by beauty!"

They blushed prettily.

"Gomez Addams," Flora said.

"You terrible flirt," Fauna said.

"Always was," Flora said.

Fauna nodded. "At least with me . . . ."

Flora frowned at her. "Copycat!" she said.

"Tagalong!" Fauna retorted.

Morticia came gliding over in her sweeping dress.

"Why, Gomez," she said. "The Amor twins. I've heard so much about you."

"Morticia! I hate you!" Flora said, smiling.

"You nabbed him, this darling man . . ." Fauna said.

Flora moved possessively closer to Gomez. "He was mine."

"He was *mine*," Fauna said.

Ever tactful, Morticia stepped in. "Flora, Fauna, how can I compete? You're twice the woman I am."

Tully was striding by, in search of Margaret, and Gomez grabbed him.

"Tully, the Amor twins," he said. "They're waiting for Fester. Amuse them."

Flora batted her eyes flirtatiously. "Hello, Tully."

"*I* saw him first," Fauna said.

"Ignore her," Flora said to Tully.

"She's nothing," Fauna said.

The girls now had their four arms all over Tully, leading him to the dance floor. He threw a stricken look back over his shoulder at Morticia and Gomez.

"*Bonne chance!*" Morticia said, and she and Gomez danced away together.

Abigail was still up in Fester's bedroom, alone. Fester came in, climbing through the open window, looking very upset.

"I can't find her anywhere," he said, out of breath. "Let's just leave — out the back."

"Pull yourself together," Abigail ordered. "She'll

turn up, the little cockroach. Now, get to the party, or they'll suspect something. I'll be down soon." She put on her Germanic accent. "Ja?"

Fester hung his head. "Yes, Mother," he said, and headed for the stairs.

Chapter 19

In the kitchen, Morticia watched as Granny garnished a roast pig set on a silver tray. It was beautifully glazed, deliciously plump, and had a bright red apple in its mouth.

"Mama, you've outdone yourself," Morticia said.

Granny turned the pig slightly to arrange the garnish, revealing its second head. That head, also, had an apple in its mouth.

"Hey, it's a party," she said, and covered the pig with a just-polished silver lid.

Then, she nodded at Lurch, who lifted the tray onto a small cart, and rolled the cart out to serve their guests.

Flora and Fauna, dancing with Tully, chattered giddily as he tried to maneuver them through a box step.

"You can't imagine how surprised we were when Gomez called and told us Fester was back," Flora said.

Fauna bobbed her head in a nod. "Especially considering . . ." She stopped, and gave her sister a significant look.

"Fauna . . ." Flora said, and rolled her eyes heavenward.

"Especially considering what?" Tully asked, curiosity aroused.

Flora and Fauna looked at each other.

"It makes no difference now," Flora said. "It's obvious that Fester and Gomez are devoted."

"Why wouldn't they be devoted?" Tully asked.

"Well," Fauna said, and lowered her voice so that they wouldn't be overheard. "Now that Fester's back, he's king of the castle again, isn't he?"

Tully looked confused.

"Fester's the older brother," Flora explained. "So he gets it all. The house, the money — you name it."

"*Everything?*" Tully asked.

Flora nodded.

Fauna smiled, slyly. "Fester's still single, isn't he . . .?"

"Are *you*, Mr. Alford?" Flora asked, batting her eyelashes a few more times.

"Why, Fauna," Tully said, pretending to be shocked.

"I'm Fauna!" Fauna said.

"I'm Flora!" Flora said.

"And *I'm* flattered," Tully said. "Excuse me, ladies?" He winked at Flora, blew a kiss at Fauna, and they both giggled madly.

Then he hurried off, grinning like the cat who swallowed the canary.

* * *

Morticia and Fester appeared at the door to the ballroom.

"Everyone, your attention, please," Morticia said.

The music stopped instantly, the guests falling silent.

"When he was lost, our family grieved," Morticia said. "And how it became them." She smiled. "Now he is found, and our celebration begins. Our treasured guest of honor — Fester Addams!"

She took him by the hand as if to lead him towards the assembled guests but, instead, spun him by the arm, sending him whirling like a top into the center of the dance floor, where he stopped, nose-to-nose with Gomez.

Gomez, who was now dressed like Hollywood's version of a cossack, was carrying five gleaming scimitars.

"The mamushka!" he said, and began to circle around Fester, as Morticia, Granny, and all of the Addams women rapped out a stirring martial beat on tambourines.

As Gomez circled, the other family members formed a ring, circling counterclockwise. Gomez then threw the scimitars straight up, high in the air, and began juggling them.

Baffled, Fester stood in the center of the circle, the eye of this dizzying hurricane.

"Taught to us by our cossack cousins," Gomez said, juggling, "the masmushka has been an Addams family tradition since who knows when. . . ."

He hurled the scimitars to Fester, and they began juggling back and forth — much to Fester's shock and surprise.

"We danced the mamushka while Nero fiddled!" Gomez said, without missing a beat. "We danced the mamushka at Waterloo! We danced the mamushka for Jack the Ripper, and now, Fester Addams, this mamushka's for you!"

The juggling continued, the moves getting more and more intricate. It was an elaborate, carefully choreographed routine, and Fester — petrified — managed somehow to bungle his way through.

Then they launched into a tongue-twisting patter song, Fester stumbling through it. During an instrumental section of the song, Gomez smiled over at him.

"After all this time," he shouted to the crowd, "Fester hasn't forgotten a step, hasn't forgotten a word!"

Fester stopped dead. "Not a step, not a word," he said, astonished. He looked up to see all five scimitars dropping fast, coming straight at him.

Panicking, he caught . . . one, two, three, four — with two in each hand, his hands were full, and there was still one more — and he opened his mouth to scream, and the scimitar dropped straight in, Fester swallowing it to the hilt.

The Addams mob cheered lustily, and launched into the finale of the song.

Amazed, Fester dropped the scimitars he was holding, and pulled the other one from his mouth.

"How did I do that?" he said aloud.

Gomez slapped him on the back, and Fester burped.

Hearing that, the Addams clan cheered again — and moved in to shake this very special relative's hand.

In a remote corner of the ballroom, Cousin It and Margaret were waltzing together.

"We've been married for almost twenty years," Margaret said. "Sometimes it seems like more . . ."

"*Ooot oot blipper*," Cousin It said sympathetically.

Margaret nodded. "Of course, people grow, people change."

"*Glipper gleep gleep*," Cousin It said.

Margaret nodded.

Out in the front hall, wearing his coat, Tully was heading for the door. Abigail, on her way downstairs, stopped him.

"Where are you going?" she asked. "There's trouble."

Tully grinned at her. "Hey — not to worry. Plan B."

"But that hideous little girl . . ." Abigail said.

"I'm in charge now," Tully said, interrupting her. "Ten minutes — I'll be back." He opened the door and slipped outside.

In the ballroom, a reprise of the mamushka had just begun.

* * *

Tully went straight over to Judge Womack's house. Judge Womack was in an apoplectic mood, as the raucous sounds of the mamushka reverberated from the Addams mansion.

"What's going on over there?" he demanded, arms across his chest, staring down at the house.

"How would you like to be rid of the Addamses for good?" Tully asked. "I'm serious."

Judge Womack's face broke into a smile. "What can I do for you?" he asked.

Chapter 20

It was two in the morning, and Gomez and Morticia stood on the front steps, waving good-bye to their departing guests.

Cousin It leaned out the window of his limousine, sharing a romantic last moment with Margaret.

"You're a marvelous dancer," she said. "It's been such fun."

"*Ooot ooot gibber,*" Cousin It said.

Margaret looked torn. "I can't. We mustn't." She paused. "Call me?"

The limo drove off, Margaret waving a fond farewell.

Morticia walked down to join her.

"Oh, Margaret," she said, putting her arm around her. "He's very special, isn't he?"

Margaret sighed, watching the limo disappear into the darkness. "He's perfect," she said.

Morticia nodded, understanding. "He's It," she said simply.

Flora and Fauna were giving good-bye kisses to Fester, covering him with lipstick, hanging onto him with all four arms. Fester was enjoying this very much.

"You'll come see me before you leave, won't you, Fester?" Flora asked.

"I'll call," Fauna told him, confidentially, "once I'm alone."

An ambulance pulled up, and white-jacketed attendants stepped out with a straitjacket built for two.

"There's your ride!" Fester said. "Good-bye, girls!"

Once he had seen them off, he went upstairs, skipping down the hall, still practicing bits of the mamushka. He danced into his room, where Abigail was waiting, and started dancing with her, singing the patter song.

She just stared at him, and he stopped.

"Mother, I — I'm so terribly sorry," he said. "It was just a party. It's over. It means nothing."

Abigail clutched him in a savage hug. "Say it, Gordon. Make me believe it."

"I love you," Fester said. "And I want money."

Appeased, Abigail released him.

"Come on. We've got to go find Tully," she said.

Morticia went to the ballroom, looking for her children. She discovered Pugsley asleep, curled up on the silver platter where the two-headed pig had been. She found this enchanting.

As Gomez came in, she hushed him, pointing to the platter.

"Look," she whispered. "Our little boy."

"All tuckered out," Gomez said.

"So sweet," Morticia whispered. "He looks just like . . . a little entrée."

Pugsley woke up, looking around. "Where — where's the party?" he asked sleepily.

"It's over, darling," Morticia said. "Have you seen your sister?"

Pugsley shook his head. "Not since before the mamushka."

Morticia glanced at Gomez, very worried. "Have you?"

"Don't fret," Gomez said. "We'll find her."

In no time, he had rallied the entire family for a search. Granny had grabbed her divining rod, and Lurch distributed torches, as Pugsley helped Gomez unroll an ancient map of the area. Morticia just stood, shivering, in her black cloak.

"Fan out," Gomez said. "Pugsley — head for the dung heap. Mama and Morticia — the shallow graves. I'll take the abyss, and Lurch — check the bottomless pit."

Morticia's face paled even more. "Her favorite . . ."

"Fester!" Gomez said, looking around.

"Up here," Fester said, from his bedroom window.

"Fester — you take the ravine!" Gomez said. "And the unmarked, abandoned well!"

Fester shook his head, guiltily. "Someone should stay behind — in case she comes back."

Gomez considered that, then nodded. "Good man! Good thinking!"

"Who's going to take the swamp?" Granny asked.

Thing tugged at the cuff of Gomez' pants.

"That's the spirit, Thing — lend a hand!" Gomez said. "Come on, everyone. Let's go!"

They all swept out into the night, with Gomez in the lead.

Upstairs, Abigail came to stand with Fester at the window, and they watched the family members spread far and wide over the grounds, holding tiny lights aloft as they searched for Wednesday.

"Where is Tully?" Abigail asked. "We must find him."

Fester sighed, then nodded and followed her.

It took a while, but they found him in the den, sitting in an armchair, basking in the rays of sunshine that beamed from a copy of *The Sun Also Rises*.

"What are you doing?" Abigail asked.

"Relaxing." Tully smiled. "Taking a little sun."

"Have you gone mad?" Abigail asked.

"*Au contraire*." Tully closed the book, and smugly unfurled a legal document for them to see.

The family continued searching, without success, for Wednesday.

Thing hopped from lily pad to lily pad, stopping occasionally to look for signs of his mistress, while over in the primeval forest, Pugsley wandered, calling for his sister, holding his torch high in the air.

Lurch went out into the neighborhood, picking

up parked cars, and looking for Wednesday underneath them.

Morticia and Granny were in the underground grotto, standing in the middle of the dripping dankness, stalagmites and stalactites all around them. Granny waved her torch, and scary shadows leapt on the cave walls.

"Wednesday!" she called. "Wednesday!"

Morticia was close to tears. "Oh, Mama, I was sure we'd find her here."

Gomez was in the cemetery, going through the mausoleums. He ventured into one at the far end, where two proud marble vultures guarded the entryway. Gomez lowered the uplifted claw of one of the vultures, and the stone doors slid open.

Inside, it was catacomblike, filled with the bleached bones of the Addams dead. Gomez' torch cast shadows, one of which belonged to Wednesday, who was curled asleep on a stone sarcophagus.

Relieved to find her, Gomez approached quietly so he wouldn't wake her up. Tenderly, he lifted her into his arms.

He had been more worried than he wanted to admit.

He summoned the rest of the family, and they formed a triumphant procession back to the house, Lurch carrying the sleeping Wednesday and Pugsley.

But, when they got there, Gate wouldn't — *couldn't* — open. It rattled miserably on its hinges, locked tight with heavy chains and yellow police tape. A large NO TRESPASSING! COURT ORDER! ADDAMS FAMILY — KEEP OUT!!! sign was posted on its rusty bars.

The Addams family stopped in horror.

They had been banned from their own house.

Chapter 21

"What's all this?" Gomez demanded as Tully came down the walkway, waving his legal document.

"This," Tully said, "is a restraining order, Gomez."

Gomez looked at him blankly. "A restraining order?"

"It requires you to keep a distance of one thousand yards from this house," Tully said, his voice dripping with smug confidence. "You've got about nine hundred and ninety-nine yards to go — catch my drift?"

"I am restrained — from my own house?" Gomez asked, in complete disbelief.

Tully smiled. "Not *your* house, moustache! Not anymore! It belongs to the eldest living descendant, the older of the brothers — Fester Adams!"

"But — " Gomez shook his head, trying to take this in. "This is lunacy!"

"Fester adores Gomez," Morticia said, just as stunned.

"No," Tully said. "He's afraid of him. Seeing the

twins brought it all back." He gave his former client a toothy grin. "You're bitter rivals, Gomez — always were, always will be!"

"It's not so!" Gomez protested. "Those girls meant nothing to me — he knows that. I demand to see Fester!"

Tully shook his head, leaning arrogantly on Gate. "Sorry, no can do," he said. "He's very hurt — it's not a good time. Leave it alone. Or, better yet — just *leave*."

Wednesday came forward, rubbing sleep out of her eyes. "But, he isn't even Uncle Fester," she said.

Gomez and Morticia turned to look at her, then looked at each other, their former worst suspicions confirmed.

"Do not fear," Gomez said to the rest of the family. "Justice shall prevail. The courts will decide!" He held a determined fist up in the air. "They say a man who represents himself has a fool for a client. Well," he shook his fist, "*I am that fool!*"

In court the next day, Judge Womack was the presiding judge. After barely listening to both sides, he hammered his gavel on the bench, ready to render his decision.

"Given applicable standards of proof," he said pompously, "the attempts to impugn this man's character" — he indicated Fester — "or question his identity have been woefully inadequate. It is with no small amount of personal satisfaction that

I declare Fester Addams legal executor of the Addams estate, and rightful owner of all properties and possessions contained herein. Gomez Addams . . ." He held up a golf ball, smiling unpleasantly. "I believe this is yours."

The family was stunned.

Justice had *not* prevailed.

They were allowed to go back to the house to pack a paltry few possessions, which they carried out to the car. Gomez was already sitting in the passenger seat, his head thrown back in abject misery, his coat draped across his shoulders as though he were an invalid.

Morticia lugged out Cleo, her carnivorous plant, and Granny brought her favorite cauldron. Wednesday had one of her Marie Antoinette dolls, and Pugsley had his chemistry set under one arm. Lurch uprooted his favorite tree and joined the others. Thing brought up the rear, dragging a toy wagon packed with his rings and his glove.

Then, the Duesenberg eased out of the driveway and onto the street, weighed down by Lurch's tree, which was sticking out of the trunk.

Fester, standing at a second-story window, watched the car drive off, completely expressionless.

The Addams family drove to nearby Wampum Court to rent a bungalow. There was a bright neon two-way arrow pointing the way to the bungalows, which were built in a horrible ersatz western style. Log cabins of simulated wood surrounded the teepee-shaped office.

After checking in, they parked down at the farthest cabin. Lurch ripped up the asphalt in big chunks to park his tree.

The interior of the cabin was decorated with a cowboy-and-Indian motif, mixed with chrome-plated plastic, and there was a thick orange shag carpet on the floor. The first thing Morticia did was hang up a picture she had brought from the mansion. Then, she stepped back to admire her handiwork.

Granny gave her a consoling pat on the back. "I like it," she said.

Morticia nodded bravely. "Just as long as we're all together, *n'est-ce pas, mon cher?*"

Gomez sat slumped in a chair made from a wagon wheel and Naugahyde. He looked as though all of the insane, vibrant energy had been completely drained out of his body.

"*N'est-ce pas, mon cher?*" Morticia said again.

Gomez looked up as though he had never heard French in his life. "Hunh?"

Wednesday pressed a cool washcloth to his forehead, giving her mother a worried look.

Pugsley came out from the bathroom, nibbling a wrapped bar of motel soap.

"This place isn't half bad," he said, with his mouth full. "They even put candy in the bathroom."

"That's the soap, dear," Morticia said.

"Oh," Pugsley said, shrugged, and took another greedy bite.

Wednesday put her hand on her father's arm. "Do you want a cigar, Father?"

"They're very bad for you," Gomez said in a monotone.

"Father?" Wednesday said, and exchanged a panic-stricken look with Morticia.

The whole family moved closer to him.

"But, maybe I'll have one of those," Gomez said, taking a bar of soap from Pugsley. He unwrapped it, and began morosely eating.

He was a broken shell of a man.

Chapter 22

At the Addams mansion, Abigail, Fester, and Tully were trying to get into the vault — but they couldn't get past the room of countless hanging chains. Over and over, they each took a chain and pulled, and over and over, something bad happened.

As, once again, the coal chute on the side of the house dropped open, dumping the three of them out in a wet and bedraggled heap, Abigail scowled at her son.

"You're doing this on purpose," she said.

Fester just coughed out water, and tried to catch his breath.

They all struggled to their feet and marched grimly back into the house to try again.

Gomez felt even worse in the morning. He lay stretched out on the bare box springs of his bed, the mattress pushed aside. A damp cloth covered his eyes, and Thing massaged his aching head. There was a bowl of motel soaps beside him, which he munched, miserably.

In contrast, Morticia was squarely facing the crisis. She addressed the rest of the family from the head of the breakfast table, the want ads open in front of her.

"We are the Addamses, and we will not submit," she said. "Who recalls the tale of the tortoise and the hare? The swift, yet lazy little cottontail, and his slow but determined companion? What does that story teach us, as Addamses?"

Everyone else exchanged uncertain glances.

"Kill the hare," Granny said finally. "Skin it. Boil it."

"Put the tortoise on the highway," Wednesday said.

Pugsley nodded. "During rush hour."

Morticia smiled at all of them, very pleased by their grasp of the story. "Yes!" she said. "We will survive! Poison us, strangle us, break our bones — we will come back for more. And why?"

"Because we like it!" Granny said.

"Because we're Addamses!" Pugsley said, infected by their enthusiasm.

Gomez tried to rouse himself, sitting up partway. "We're Addamses," he said, dully, and then burped, soap bubbles floating from his mouth.

The rest of the family sighed.

But, following Morticia's example, they all got to work. Wednesday and Pugsley set up a refreshment stand, their contribution to the Addamses' financial well-being. They had an array of poisons lined up on their rickety table. To try and drum up business, they had slashed their prices to a nickel a cup.

Cars sped by, without even slowing down.

Carrying a sample vacuum cleaner and a bucket, Lurch came out of the motel courtyard.

Pugsley poured him a cup of punch from the steaming pitcher. "Here, Lurch," he said. "On the house."

Lurch downed it in a gulp, and headed off. Then, feeling the effects of the brew, he opened his mouth, a tongue of flame shooting out and incinerating a wooden Indian advertising the Wampum Court. Lurch just shrugged, and continued on his way.

Morticia had gone straight down to the employment agency, where a relentlessly perky personnel officer interviewed her.

"We have so many homemakers reentering the work force," the personnel officer said. "Your domestic skills can be very valuable. College?"

"Private tutors," Morticia answered.

The personnel officer nodded, writing that on her clipboard. "Major?"

"Spells and Hexes," Morticia said.

"Liberal arts," the personnel officer said, with a knowing nod. "Have you been a volunteer? PTA, service organizations?"

"Well." Morticia thought that over. "One day each week, I visit death row at our local prison, with my children."

The personnel officer looked perplexed. "With your children?"

Morticia nodded. "Autographs."

The personnel officer blinked. "Well," she said, without missing a beat. "What about your husband? Is he currently employed?"

"He's . . . he's going through a bad patch at the moment," Morticia said. "But it's not his fault."

"Of course not," the personnel officer said, more than a little bitter. "What is he — a loafer? A hopeless layabout? A shiftless dreamer?"

"Not anymore," Morticia said wistfully.

The personnel officer shot her a doubtful glance, then began rifling through her jobs file.

Wednesday and Pugsley were still at their refreshment stand. They were negotiating with a prissy little girl in a Girl Scout uniform.

"Is this made with real lemons?" the Girl Scout asked, looking dubiously at the pitcher.

"Yes," Wednesday said, her face perfectly straight.

The Girl Scout sniffed at the liquid, then stepped back. "I only like all-natural foods and beverages," she said. "Organically grown, with no preservatives. Are you *sure* they're real lemons?"

"*Yes*," Pugsley said, losing patience.

"Tell you what," the Girl Scout said, taking out a box of cookies. "I'll buy a cup, if you buy a box of my delicious Girl Scout cookies. Do we have a deal?"

"Well" — Wednesday frowned — "are they made from real Girl Scouts?"

Lurch stopped in front of a lovely white clapboard suburban house. There were geraniums in beautifully tended flower boxes, and the property was surrounded by a white picket fence.

Carrying his sample vacuum cleaner and bucket, the tools of his new trade, Lurch carefully opened the little white gate. Then, he rang the doorbell, trying not to break anything.

A blonde housewife in tennis whites, obviously in a hurry, opened the door, only to be greeted by a bucketfull of slop thrown past her, onto the peach Oriental rug. She screamed in horror, turned to challenge the perpetrator of this atrocity and, seeing Lurch, screamed again.

In a panic, she tried to slam the door, but as the salesman's manual had advised, Lurch stuck his foot in the way, the door partially ripping off its hinges. He withdrew his foot and stepped inside, shutting the door as well as he could.

After a minute, he came back out, jauntily waving a check.

He loved being a butler, but perhaps door-to-door sales was his true calling.

Morticia had been assigned to a day-care center as a mother's helper. She sat on a low chair, telling a story to a circle of toddlers perched on small carpet squares. The room was sunny and cheerful, with crayon drawings taped to the walls.

". . . and so," Morticia said, "the witch lured Hansel and Gretel into the candy house, by promising them more sweets. And she told them to look in the oven, and she was about to push them in, when, lo and behold, Hansel pushed the poor, defenseless witch into the oven instead. Where she was burned alive, writhing in agony." She smiled at the children. "Now, boys and girls, what do you think that feels like?"

The toddlers began loudly crying and wailing.

Morticia smiled again. It had been a while since she had told stories to tiny children, but, clearly, she had not lost the knack.

Back at the bungalow, Granny was trying to get dinner ready. She held a club behind her back, stalking something in the woods next to the cabin.

"Here, kitty, kitty, kitty . . ." she said softly.

Inside, eating compulsively from a box of Mallomars, Gomez was still stretched out on the naked box spring. He stared vacantly at a game show on TV — *Jeopardy*.

"Monsters of History for two hundred dollars," Alex Trebek read from a card. "He was known as the 'Butcher of Bavaria.' "

"Grandfather Addams!" Gomez shouted, then smacked himself on the forehead. "Drat! Not in the *form* of a question!"

Granny, running now, her club raised, hurried past the open window. She stopped at the sight of Gomez inside.

He had changed the channel and was now standing on the bed, staring at Sally Jesse Raphaël's talk show.

"Voodoo zombies — the stuff of legend, or a living nightmare?" Sally was saying, in her opening promo. "Do zombies really exist? How are they made? Where can we find them? Call in with your comments."

A call-in number flashed on the screen, and Gomez, his eyes glazed, reached for the telephone.

Granny turned away from the window. It was just too horrible to watch.

Chapter 23

At the Addams mansion, Abigail and Fester were seated at opposite ends of the table in the dining room, having lunch. The house was very quiet.

"After lunch, we'll try again," Abigail said.

"Yes, Mother," Fester answered, his voice very flat.

"We'll find the money," Abigail said. "And meanwhile, we'll have this little nest. Quiet and cozy. Without that dreadful family."

Fester nodded. "Yes, Mother."

"Just the two of us," Abigail said, a little desperately. "Away from the world. Our dream come true."

"Yes, Mother," Fester said, in his drone, and stared down at his untouched lunch.

In the bungalow, Sally Jesse Raphaël was still on — and talking to a woman in the studio audience.

"So, your son was brainwashed by voodoo slave masters," she said, looking concerned, "and forced to recruit others. Wow. Let's take a call."

Gomez' voice burst out on the studio PA system. "Sally . . ."

Sally Jesse frowned up at the sound. "Mr. Addams, *please* stop calling," she said. "We don't know where they meet."

In the motel room, Gomez let the phone fall from his hand. Morticia, seated on the edge of the box spring, tried to comfort him. Pugsley, Wednesday, and Lurch were in nearby chairs, looking very upset, as though at a death watch.

Gomez was now surrounded by junk food, and a mountain of junk food wrappers, bags, and Styrofoam containers.

Ritually, as handmaidens, Morticia brought Gomez the remote control for the television, and Wednesday brought him a copy of *TV Guide*. Pugsley gave him a bag of Doritos, and Lurch handed him a canister of Pringles.

Gomez nodded his thanks, and used the remote to switch channels; an episode of *The Cosby Show* flashed on.

"Rerun," he said grimly and switched off the set, staring at the blank screen.

"I don't understand," Pugsley whispered. "All he does is watch TV and eat."

Morticia jumped to her feet. "I know! Gomez, let's go for a drive. The whole family."

Gomez didn't even look up. "A drive?" he said. "And miss *Matlock*?"

Granny opened the door, sticking her head in.

"Dinner's going to be late," she said, then

slammed the door and started whistling. "Here, boy. Here, boy."

It was later that night, and Morticia was putting Wednesday to bed.

"If that man isn't Uncle Fester, then who is he, Mother?" Wednesday asked, wide awake and worried.

"I don't know, darling." Morticia sighed, tucking her in. "I wish I did."

"Why is that lady doing all this?" Wednesday asked.

"It's hard to say." Morticia tried to think of a good explanation. "Sometimes, people have had terrible childhoods. And sometimes, they just haven't found their special place in life. And sometimes, they're just wicked and must be destroyed."

With that, she bent down and kissed Wednesday, who closed her eyes to go to sleep.

Soon, the whole family was asleep, except for Morticia. Wednesday was in the same bed as Granny, and Lurch was flat out on the floor. Pugsley was using him for a mattress, and Thing was using Pugsley for a mattress. Pugsley snored the inhale part of a snore, Lurch groaned the exhale, and Thing punctuated the snore by wiggling.

Morticia stared down at the restlessly sleeping Gomez for a long minute, stroking his hair lovingly. Then, full of resolve, she got out of bed.

She put on her cloak and went outside, walking

away from the hotel. Unseen by her, Thing trailed along behind.

When she got to what had been their house, she struggled with Gate, trying to get it to open, as Thing clutched the bars, also attempting to block her way.

"Stop it, you two," Morticia said, and she broke free of Thing, and pushed through Gate.

When she knocked on the front door, Tully answered it, smiling maliciously when he saw her.

"I would like to speak to Fester," Morticia said.

Tully stepped aside. "We have been expecting you . . ." he said, and smiled an evil smile.

Morticia nodded, and crossed the threshold.

Back at Gate, Thing was beside himself. Finally, he scampered down to the intersection at the foot of the Addams hill. He did his best to flag down any of the few oncoming cars, waving to no avail. He danced around in frustration, then tried hitchhiking, sticking out his thumb.

A passing car promptly splashed him with mud.

Screwing up his courage, in a kamikaze leap, Thing grabbed hold of the bumper of the next car that came along and hung on for dear life as the car sped down the street.

He had to go tell the others.

In no time, Morticia had been stretched out on the torture rack in the study, Tully and Fester securing her hands and her feet, under Abigail's supervision. Fester was following orders reluctantly, torn and agitated.

"You are a desperate woman, consumed by greed and infinite bitterness," Morticia said graciously to Abigail, then paused. "We could have been such friends."

"I don't think so," Abigail said, her voice almost as unpleasant as her expression. "The vault, Mrs. Addams — any thoughts?"

"Despite everything," Morticia said sweetly, "I don't hate you. I pity you. Persecution, fiendish torture, inhuman depravity — sometimes it's just not enough."

Abigail frowned at her and turned to Fester. "Gordon, let's get started," she said.

Fester shifted his weight from one foot to the other. "But, Mother," he said, glancing guiltily at Morticia for a second.

"Stop stalling!" Abigail said.

"I'm not stalling!" Fester shifted his weight. "Stop badgering me!"

Giving up, Abigail pushed him aside.

"Tully, take over!" she ordered. "Tighten it!"

Tully looked squeamish. "I'd love to," he said, "you know that, but — I've got this stomach thing. When I torture people. It's just me."

Abigail shoved him towards the rack. "Do it!"

Tully looked at Morticia. "Uh, where's your bathroom?" he asked politely.

"Now!" Abigail said, her voice crackling with authority.

Tully shut his eyes and tightened the rack. Morticia's bones made a horrible popping, stretching sound. Instead of screaming, Morticia moaned happily.

"Again!" Abigail said.

Tully tightened the rack, and there were more bone-popping noises. Morticia moaned joyfully.

Abigail frowned. "Harder!"

Tully tightened the rack a third time.

Morticia moaned, more joyfully than ever, then winked at Tully. "You've done this before, haven't you," she said.

A hand possessed, Thing raced up the driveway of Wampum Court, raising dust as he went. He leapt onto the porch, then knocked on the cabin door.

"Who is it?" Gomez asked sleepily. "We're paid through Thursday."

Thing pounded on the door, and Gomez opened it. Thing rushed in. He skittered on the kitchen counter, frantically signing to Gomez, as the rest of the family slept.

"Slow down, Thing!" Gomez whispered. "It's terrible when you stutter!"

Thing grabbed a spoon, and began tapping out Morse code.

" 'Morticia in danger . . . stop'!" Gomez translated. " 'Send help at once . . . stop'! "

Thing flopped down in exhausted triumph.

"Come on!" Gomez said, grabbed him, and ran out of the bungalow.

Chapter 24

Since the rack hadn't worked, Tully and Abigail lashed Morticia to an enormous torture wheel, then went over to the fireplace to tend the branding irons stuck in the roaring fire.

"You can't!" Fester protested. "Not with red-hot pokers!"

Tully looked sick to his stomach again. "Is this gonna smell?"

"Tully Alford — charlatan. Deadbeat. Parasite," Morticia said, with gracious understanding. "How Gomez adored you."

"Well, not enough," Tully said, and pushed the poker further into the fire to heat it up.

Fester wrung his hands together frantically. "Morticia, please. . . . Tell them."

"Dear Fester — or whoever you are," Morticia said, smiling at him. "Which is the real you — the loathsome, underhanded monster you've become? Or the loathsome underhanded monster we came to love?"

"I don't know anymore. Don't ask me," Fester said desperately.

Now, a horrible smirk spread over Abigail's face. "Gordon, I have a thought," she said. "Just a notion, top of my head. Tell me what you think. Since you and Mrs. Addams are so very close. . . ." She took a red-hot poker out of the fire and handed it to him. "Be my guest."

Gomez cut the engine of the Duesenberg, and the car drove quietly through Gate, who opened without the slightest creak. Gomez stopped the car and skulked out, Thing skulking after him.

Seeing the reflection of the roaring fire through the study window, Gomez looked in to see Fester take the poker and approach Morticia. Instantly, Gomez crashed through the window in a back flip, Thing judo-flipping in after him.

"*Cara mia!*" Gomez said, landing on his feet.

Morticia smiled at him from the torture wheel. "*Mon cher!*"

Abigail gasped. "Addams!"

Thing tossed Gomez a saber off the study wall, and Tully also grabbed a saber, approaching Gomez from behind.

"Darling, take care!" Morticia said, motioning with her head, since she was unable to point with her hands lashed down.

Without even looking, Gomez parried Tully's blow from behind.

"Dirty pool, old man," he said. "Never again!"

Tully nodded. "This is for keeps, Gomez! Not just

doubloons!" He feinted, then slashed, cutting the front of Gomez' jacket to pieces.

"One for you, Tully — " Gomez attacked, his blade flashing.

In a blur of action, Tully's sword was knocked from his hand and he was sent tumbling backwards, landing on his knees.

"And one for me!" Gomez finished and raised his sword.

Tully looked up at him with cowardly, pleading eyes. "Gomez, it's Tully. I'm your lawyer. I'm on *retainer*."

Gomez hesitated.

"Let him up!" Abigail said, from behind him.

Gomez turned, sword in hand, to see Abigail, who now had a pistol. She was aiming it at Morticia.

One shot, and Morticia would die a horrible death.

Without hesitation, Gomez threw aside his sword.

"That's right," Abigail said, as Tully scrambled to his feet. "Now get moving — Addams, take him to the vault. And if you're not back in one hour . . ." She gestured with the pistol at Morticia. "I *displace* her."

Gomez was close enough to take Morticia's hand on the torture wheel.

"Tish — seeing you like this," he said. "My blood boils."

"As does mine," Morticia said, gripping his hand tightly.

Gomez touched the torture wheel with his other

hand. "This wheel of pain . . ." he said sadly.

"*Our* wheel," Morticia said.

Gomez nodded. "To live without you, darling — only that would be torture."

"A day alone, *mon cher*," Morticia said. "Only *that* would be death."

Gomez bent, and kissed her hand.

"Knock it off!" Abigail said. "The vault, Addams — right now!"

Gomez reached for the book that would open the secret panel.

"But, Mother," Fester spoke up tentatively, "can't we — "

"Can it, Gordon!" Abigail said, scowling at him. "Stop dragging your feet! You disgust me — you're nothing but a useless, sniveling baby! A stone around my neck! What was I thinking? I should have left you where I found you!"

As these words sunk in, Fester sprang forward.

"No tricks, Gomez!" he said. "That's the wrong book!"

Gomez's hand was on the right book, *Greed*, but Fester stopped him from pulling it.

"Allow me," Fester said.

Gomez looked into Fester's eyes, realizing what he was about to do.

"Good show, old man," he murmured, and stepped aside.

Fester reached for a different book — *Hurricane Irene: Nightmare from Above*.

Seeing the title, Tully suddenly panicked. "Put

that book down, Gordon! You don't know what it can do! It's not just — literature!"

"Oh, really?" Fester said, advancing on him.

Tully backed up. "I-I'm your friend, Gordon — think of the doubloons!"

"They're not yours, Tully!" Fester said, holding the book threateningly.

While everyone else was distracted, Gomez moved to release Morticia from the torture wheel.

"Quickly, my darling!" she said.

He helped her down, shaking with fury. "Leather straps, red-hot pokers — "

"Later, my dearest," Morticia promised.

Tully was cowering on the floor, and Abigail moved into a face-off with Fester.

"Keep that book closed, Gordon," she said sharply. "Listen to Mother!"

Fester shook his head. "I'll never listen to you — not ever again!"

Abigail spoke more softly now, putting on her nicest smile. "I had to be strict with you — because I cared," she said. "Put it down!"

Fester shook his head, hanging onto the book. "You never really loved me!" he said. "Now, I know it!"

Gomez took Morticia's hand. "Come, my love — to safety!"

Morticia hung back for a second. "But, what of Fester?" she asked.

"Old man, this way!" Gomez yelled, motioning to his brother.

Fester looked at him, then looked back at Abigail. "You're a terrible mother! There, I said it!" He opened the book, and blasted Tully out of the window, then blasted Abigail out as well.

Gomez yanked *Greed* out of the bookcase to open the secret chamber. Amid the storm, he led Morticia behind the bookshelf, and tried to hold it open for Fester to follow, fighting the gale-force winds.

"Old man!" he shouted as loudly as he could. "This way!"

Thing struggled across the floor to the bookshelf, the wind pelting him with papers and other flying debris. Just as he crawled to safety, Gomez could no longer fight the powerful winds and the bookshelf slammed shut.

Fester tried to close the book to quell the storm, but a huge bolt of lightning zapped him first. He fell to the floor, twisting and writhing, electricity coursing wildly through his body.

Then, it was dark.

Chapter 25

It was October, and a group of little children approached the front door of the Addamses' mansion. There was a hand-lettered sign on the door reading: HALLOWEEN OPEN HOUSE. The children, dressed in traditional Halloween costumes and carrying trick-or-treat bags, giggled and chattered. One of them — a small witch — stepped forward and knocked on the door.

As it opened, they chanted, "Trick or — " They froze in midchant and ran screaming away, back out to the street.

Lurch closed the front door, looking puzzled.

The family was busily decorating the house for their annual Halloween festivities. The crystal globes in the chandeliers had been replaced by miniature jack-o'-lanterns, and skeletons, each wearing a top hat, hung from the sconces by nooses around their necks. There were clusters of black and orange balloons everywhere, covered with cobwebs.

Together, Uncle Fester and Thing were draping the banisters with a garland made from crepe paper, dead branches, and Spanish moss. Gomez hung up-side down from the balcony as Morticia handed him another decoration to put up.

Skulls, each holding a candle, were scattered about, and a stuffed scarecrow leaned against the staircase, with a pitchfork through its throat. A banner on the wall read HAPPY HALLOWEEN, and the letters dripped with blood.

Granny came out of the kitchen, carrying a tray of food for the trick-or-treaters. When she saw that they were gone, she just shrugged.

"Well, it's their loss," she said. "I even made finger sandwiches."

"Here we are!" Pugsley announced, and he and Wednesday came down the stairs.

Wednesday was dressed in her usual style, but Pugsley was dressed as a tiny version of Uncle Fester, complete with bald head and greatcoat.

The adults were delighted to see them.

Gomez flipped down off the balcony, onto his feet. "Pugsley, old man!"

"Look at you," Morticia marveled.

Pugsley smiled up at Uncle Fester. "How do you like it?"

Fester was deeply touched, and he picked up Pugsley.

"What can I say?" He hugged him. "He's going to break hearts."

"Let's get a picture!" Gomez said.

"Oh, yes," Morticia agreed. "In the den."

There was a knock on the door, and Lurch opened it.

Standing outside were Margaret and Cousin It. Margaret was dressed as a fairy princess, complete with wand. Cousin It wore a cowboy hat, a bandanna, and a holster. Margaret was radiant, obviously very much in love.

"Trick or treat!" she said.

"*Oot oot glibber*," Cousin It said.

"Hello, Margaret," Morticia said, very pleased. "Cousin It, I almost didn't recognize you."

Margaret beamed. "Isn't he handsome? Everyone keeps asking where he bought his costume."

"It's a wonderful hat," Gomez said, admiringly.

"And what are you, darling?" Margaret asked Wednesday. "Where's your costume?"

"This *is* my costume," Wednesday said, very solemnly. "I'm a homicidal maniac. They look just like everyone else."

The family laughed appreciatively.

At Morticia's urging, they all moved to the dining room to continue the party. Lurch posed Fester and Pugsley together, then set up the easel and canvas to paint their portrait. Gomez and Wednesday sat on the floor, amid newspapers, carving a pumpkin.

Morticia worked on her knitting, while Margaret and Cousin It sat together, holding hands. Granny moved back and forth, bringing people steaming cups from the punch bowl.

"Halloween," Fester mused. "It's such a special holiday. Ghosts and goblins. Witches on broomsticks."

"Children begging in the streets," Wednesday said, and everyone else nodded blissfully.

"I'm so glad I can share this night with my family," Fester said. "My *real* family. Now that I've got my memory back."

Morticia looked up from her knitting. "That unfortunate woman. Filled with evil." She shook her head sadly. "But not enough."

"She wasn't your mother," Pugsley assured Fester. "She just *said* that."

"Ooot oot gleep?" Cousin It asked.

"You remember, old sport," Gomez said. "She really *did* find him tangled in a tuna net, twenty-five years ago. With amnesia."

Wednesday nodded gravely. "From the Bermuda Triangle."

"Ooot oot oot," Cousin It said.

"How true," Morticia agreed. "Stranger things *have* happened."

"Well." Margaret held onto Cousin It's hand with both of hers. "I'm sorry, and I'm not bitter, but I blame Tully."

"Ooot blipper gleep," Cousin It said.

"Oh, stop." Margaret tapped him with her wand coquettishly. "I'm blushing."

"Thank goodness for that lightning," Gomez said to Fester. "Knocked some sense into you."

Pugsley grinned up at him. "Please, Uncle Fester?"

"Pugsley . . ." Fester said, very jovial.

"For the picture?" Pugsley begged.

Fester popped a light bulb into his mouth — and it lit up, Pugsley giggling at the sight.

Finished with the pumpkin, Gomez placed it on

a table, then held a match to the candle inside. The pumpkin glowed. It had one eye in the middle of its forehead, and everyone *oohed* and *aahed*.

"You know," Fester said happily, "all the old sayings are true. There's no place like home. And blood *is* thicker than water."

Morticia nodded. "And just as refreshing."

Gomez clapped his hands for attention. "All right, everybody, time for a game!" he said. "What shall it be — bobbing for apples?"

"Charades?" Margaret suggested.

"*Ooot glibber glip*," Cousin It said.

"Of course." Morticia got up. " 'Wake the Dead.' "

Fester looked at Gomez with utter delight, remembering this childhood favorite. " 'Wake the Dead'!"

Gomez nodded, equally excited. " 'Wake the Dead'! Out to the cemetery! Come on, everyone!"

"I've never played this before," Margaret confided to Granny as they all headed enthusiastically outside. "How does it go?"

"Did you bring a shovel?" Granny asked.

Pugsley pulled on Fester's sleeve. "Uncle Fester, will you be on my team?"

Wednesday yanked on his other sleeve. "No, mine!"

"I'll tell you what," Fester said to Wednesday. "We'll give you a head start. Three skulls and a pelvis — how's that?"

Pugsley and Wednesday both cheered and ran outside.

Fester stopped and looked at Gomez. "My own dear brother," he said, and sighed. "What could be more precious?"

Gomez nodded. "Blood is thicker than water, old man."

"And *just* as refreshing," Morticia said, moved by the brothers' devotion.

Gomez offered his hand, and Fester took it, in a manly handshake.

"Let us never be parted," Gomez said.

"Let us always be one," Fester said, and flipped him in a judo flip.

Gomez landed at the foot of a glass display case, which contained Abigail and Tully, expertly mounted and stuffed.

"Come on!" Fester said joyfully to Gomez and Morticia. " 'Wake the Dead'!"

"We'll catch up," Morticia assured him.

Fester nodded and hurried outside after the others, leaving the two of them alone in the front hall.

"Our family," Morticia said with deep satisfaction. "What are they?"

"Oh, Tish, what a night," Gomez said. "Everyone, together at last. What more could we ask?"

Morticia smiled and held up the garment she had been knitting — a baby jumper, with three legs.

Gomez stared at her, ecstatically. *"Cara mia . . .* is it true?"

Morticia nodded. *"Oui, mon cher."*

They embraced, standing together in the open doorway.

There was a full moon. In the distance, a wolf

howled, and wispy ghosts flitted through the night sky. There was a human scream, followed by Granny's cackle, and in the cemetery torches could be seen, bobbing and flickering like fireflies.

It was the most wonderful Halloween night ever.